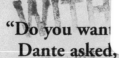

"Do you want...
Dante asked, ...
himself any longer.

His pulse spiked. He was wound up as tight as a drum from the potent combination of Adrianna's nearness and the sexual draw of her lingering question.

"Yes."

That one word was all Dante needed to hear as he closed out the bill with the bartender and helped Adrianna out of the restaurant and into his chauffeured Town Car. Once inside, his hormones switched into overdrive and one hand flew around her neck to draw her face nearer to his. Her lips were just as soft as he remembered and he pushed them apart lightly to dive inside for a taste. She tasted like heaven, and when her tongue tangled with his for supremacy, heat flooded his entire being. He pulled her close until they were chest to chest.

The kiss was so supercharged it bombarded Adrianna with the pent-up desire of ten years of not having Dante's mouth on hers. Her body was humming with the anticipation of what was to come. She'd longed for, waited, wanted this moment, and now that it was here, she intended to enjoy every minute.

Books by Yahrah St. John

Kimani Romance

Never Say Never
Risky Business of Love
Playing for Keeps
This Time for Real
If You So Desire
Two to Tango

YAHRAH ST. JOHN

is the author of eight novels and numerous short stories. A graduate of Hyde Park Career Academy, she also earned a Bachelor of Arts degree in English from Northwestern University.

Her books have garnered four-star ratings from *RT Book Reviews,* the *Rawsistaz Reviewers,* Romance in Color and numerous book clubs. A member of Romance Writers of America, St. John is an avid reader of all genres. She enjoys the arts, cooking, traveling, basketball and adventure sports, but her true passion remains writing.

St. John lives in sunny Orlando, the City Beautiful.

Two to Tango

Yahrah St. John

KIMANI
ROMANCE
TM

Dedicated to my great aunt Eloise Bishop, whose grace,
wisdom and endless spirit I admire.

 KIMANI PRESS™

ISBN-13: 978-0-373-86195-8

TWO TO TANGO

Copyright © 2011 by Yahrah Yisrael

Recycling programs
for this product may
not exist in your area.

www.kimanipress.com

Printed in U.S.A.

Dear Reader,

I hope you enjoy *Two to Tango,* the final book in the Orphan Series. Dante's story sprang from my immense love of cooking and the Food Network. I decided early on that one of the orphans had to be a chef. After tackling new love, I wanted to try a different angle with Dante by having his old flame Adrianna pop back into his life. And what better way to turn that love on its ear than a juicy secret Adrianna harbored for years and kept from Dante?

I'm currently hard at work on my ninth book about the president of a cosmetics dynasty and the corporate raider who takes over her family business.

Feel free to visit my website at www.yahrahstjohn.com for the latest updates or contact me via email at Yahrah@yahrahstjohn.com. Or become a fan on Facebook, follow me at twitter.com/yahrahstjohn or friend me at myspace.com/yahrahstjohn.

Wishing you the best,

Yahrah St. John

Acknowledgments

I would like to thank my agent Christine Witthohn
for getting me back on the map. To my dad,
Austin Mitchell, second moms Asilee Mitchell
and Beatrice Astwood, cousins Yahudiah Chodosh
and Demetrea Bishop and my entire family
for keeping me grounded.

To my fabulous sisterfriends: Tiffany Griffin,
Therolyn Rodgers, Dimitra Astwood and
Tonya Mitchell for their infectious optimism.

To my dear friends: Bhushan Sukrham, Kiara Ashanti
and coworker Melonie Hancock, for pushing me to
finish this book under a short deadline.

And a huge thanks to my fans for continuing to
support my dream.

Chapter 1

"Congratulations, Dante." Sage Anderson gave her dear friend a warm hug. Dante Moore, who was six feet tall with searing light brown eyes, a neatly trimmed goatee and dressed in a crisp white shirt open at the throat and dark slacks, was just plain fine.

She and her boyfriend, Ian Lawrence, had just arrived to their weekly family dinner at Dante's newest restaurant. Located in Harlem, Renaissance had only been open for six months, but had already hit its stride. There were several couples lined up at the door eager to get in. Lucky for them, they had reserved a private wine room and it easily accommodated their ever-expanding family.

"Thank you, Sage." Dante affectionately squeezed the five-foot-two woman who was like a little sister. She was out of her usual business suit attire and wore a rustic wrap dress that complemented her warm brown skin, short haircut and gold hoop earrings.

He glanced down at Sage and couldn't believe how far he'd come in the past seven years. When he'd been nominated for a James Beard Award for Rising Star Chef of the Year, he'd known it was time for his own place. That's when he'd opened Dante's, a tapas and wine bar in Greenwich Village. Now Renaissance was on the same path to success. Who would have ever thought that a kid who'd been abandoned by his mother as a toddler would become a successful chef and restaurateur? And thanks to Ian he was also *the* requested caterer for the crème de la crème of New York society. To be sharing this moment with the people he thought of as his family, Malik Williams, Quentin Davis, Sage and their respective partners, was the icing on the cake.

"You are truly gifted," Ian commented from Sage's side after placing a canapé in his mouth.

"Dante, you really need to be thanking Riley Ward," Malik said, "for that excellent review of up-and-coming New York restaurants in *Foodies* magazine several months back. The man positively gushed about you. You would have thought you were the Second Coming of Emeril or something." As always Malik was dressed simply in jeans and a gold T-shirt that matched his toffee complexion and dreads.

Quentin Davis held up one of the framed magazine articles currently being displayed on Renaissance's walls and read, "'Dante Moore, the Best New Chef in New York.' What a compliment!"

"And every word of it is true." Sage smiled, lightly stroking Dante's cheek.

Dante glanced back and forth at Malik, Quentin and Sage. They were his oldest and dearest friends. It was amazing that they'd all achieved their dreams given their modest beginnings at the orphanage. Quentin was a highly respected photographer; Sage, a partner at Greenberg, Waggoner, Hanson, Anderson and Associates; and Malik, the head director of the Children's Aid Network community centers in New York. And Dante was the owner of two restaurants and a thriving catering business.

"You have a point," Dante responded, stirring up the corn polenta on the table. "I think I will stop by Riley Ward's office and thank him personally." Thanks to his glowing review, their reservation list had been jam-packed for months. They also had to create a waiting list for the restaurant. He couldn't have asked for a better outcome. Initially, he'd been a little hesitant about branching out into another restaurant. He knew Greenwich Village and felt the NYU students would be major customers for Dante's, but this—classic soul dishes with a twist—was closer to his heart and gave him a chance to explore his creative side.

"When can we dig in?" Malik's wife, Peyton, asked, eyeing the hot appetizers on the table. Malik laughed at her side. Peyton was six months pregnant and the woman had a raging appetite.

"Soon, baby, soon." Malik patted Peyton's growing belly. "That son of mine is already making his presence known."

Peyton's face upturned. "And how do you know it's not a girl?" Her mocha complexion glowed from her easy pregnancy. They'd both agreed they wanted the sex of the baby to be a surprise.

Malik's chest puffed out. "It's just a feeling."

"A father's intuition?" Sage asked, chuckling.

"Call it what you will." Malik swung his dreads. "I just know."

"I hear you, Malik," Quentin replied. "I could have sworn Avery here—" he pulled his wife and baby girl nestled in her arms closer to him "—was going to have a boy, but when Bella came out wailing in the delivery room without a pee-pee, I knew I was wrong."

Everyone chuckled.

Dante glanced wistfully at his brothers who were now both happily married. Quentin and Avery already had a beautiful four-month-old baby girl and the two suited each other despite their being polar opposites. Quentin's dark good looks, broad build and bold personality versus Avery's fair complexion, slender form and conservativeness suited each other. Then there was Malik and Peyton, who had a bundle on the way. Even Sage had found herself a steady beau. Sure, Ian was ready to make an honest woman out of her, but because of his playboy past, Sage was making certain before she allowed him to put a ring on her finger. Seeing how happy they all were made Dante long for a future that would never be. A future he'd dreamed of once with Adrianna Wright before she'd walked out of his life without a word and left him with a broken heart.

"This place is certainly living up to the hype," Peyton's best friend, Amber Martin, commented as she glanced up at Dante.

Dante turned his light brown eyes on Amber. "You should know me well enough to realize that I always live up to the hype."

Amber was a looker in her snug jeans and casual top. Not to mention she was fun, hip and sassy as hell. They'd kicked it a few times a while back, but Amber was content with the single life and although Dante enjoyed her company he was ready to settle down. He wasn't looking for marriage just yet, just someone who loved him and who he could depend on.

Amber smiled widely at Dante's innuendo. She certainly did know that he lived up to it. He was a giving lover. Too bad the six-foot chef with the killer abs and dreamy bedroom eyes wanted more than she could give. Or was it the fact he was still hung up on the woman who broke his heart long ago? Whatever the case, she still considered him a friend.

"Are you two flirting?" Peyton inquired. She'd hoped for Amber to settle down with Dante a couple of years ago, but it wasn't meant to be.

"I always flirt." Amber tossed her shoulder-length hair over her shoulder. She'd allowed her former chic bob to grow out.

"She's shameless." Dante winked at Amber. "But I love her anyway." He leaned over and kissed Amber's forehead. He was happy they could still be friends even though a relationship hadn't emerged from their short time together. "Now how about we get started on dinner, before Peyton and Ian fill up on canapés?"

Ian looked up guiltily from the appetizer table. "Hey, I can't help it if your food is that good."

Dante's staff started bringing in platters of food for their weekly family dinner. Sage smiled as she watched Dante in his element. He was so warm and giving. She wished that he had someone in his life like she, Malik and Quentin had. Despite the front he put up that everything was okay, Sage recognized that Dante was lonely at times.

"How's the new art show coming along, Avery?" Dante inquired.

Avery shrugged. "Slowly. It's hard keeping so many balls in the air—the show, the gallery and being a mother to little Bella here." She reached into the bassinet on the floor and touched her daughter's cheek. "It's a balancing act."

"Much props to you, girlfriend," Amber replied. "'Cause I sure as hell couldn't do it."

"How about some coq au vin?" Dante asked, cutting the conversation short about families and babies. Something he knew nothing about.

"Sounds good to me," Malik said. "I'm starved." Since Peyton had gotten pregnant, meals at the Williams household consisted of takeout and pizza unless Malik cooked. Peyton was often too tired after teaching education courses at NYU to even think about making dinner.

For Dante, the rest of the evening continued much the same as their other family dinners. Laughter and jokes were aplenty along with some old orphanage stories tossed in for good measure, but most of all there was plenty of love. Once everyone had full bellies, eventually their tight-knit group dispersed. Quentin and Avery were the first to leave because they had to put his goddaughter, Gabrielle—Bella for short—to bed. Malik and Peyton soon followed. Only Sage, Ian and Amber were left.

"You don't have to stay, Sage," Dante said as he began piling the empty plates into a bin. Although he had staff he could call on, Dante wasn't above pitching in.

Sage was still lingering around chatting with Amber. He knew what she was up to. Sage had mentioned an associate at work that she was dying to set him up with, but she needn't worry. There wasn't a shortage of women willing to entertain him for the evening. He just hadn't found *the one*.

"I'm just waiting for Ian," Sage replied. "He went to

the kitchen so Marvin could make him a doggie bag to take home."

"Ian can afford a full-time chef ten times over, so why is he waiting on my leftovers?"

"Because," Ian replied, returning to the private wine room, "you're that good. Matter of fact—" he rubbed his chin "—I think it's time the world was introduced to you."

Dante's forehead furrowed into a frown. "What are you talking about, Ian?"

"I think it's time you had your own food show." He paused for several seconds. "On my network."

"Ohmigod!" Sage stomped her foot. "That's a fabulous idea, honey. Why didn't we think of this before?"

"Well, that is why *I'm* a multimillionaire with holdings in magazine, television and radio," Ian replied smugly, right before Sage punched him on the shoulder.

"Are you serious, Ian?" Dante asked. He was certainly intrigued. A food show would take his career to new heights.

"I never joke about money," Ian said, sternly. "Of course I'm serious. We've been toying with this idea for a few weeks now. I'll set up a meeting with my head of development and we'll discuss it."

"That sounds great." Dante stepped forward and shook Ian's hand. "Thanks for the opportunity."

"It's absolutely deserved. Sage, you ready to go?" Ian turned to his girlfriend.

"Well…" Sage paused. "I wanted to talk to Dante about something…"

"Sage, leave the man alone. He just cooked us a four-course meal, for goodness' sake," Ian returned. "Let's go home."

"All right, but you know this isn't over." Sage pointed her finger at Dante.

"Good night, Sage!" Dante waved them out of the room until it was just him and Amber.

"So…" Amber walked toward him. "How about a nightcap?"

There was no mistaking the look of hunger in Amber's eyes and it had been a while since he'd been with a woman, but Dante didn't want to give her mixed signals. He wanted a committed relationship and Amber was just not interested. "It's kind of late," Dante replied. "Another time?"

Amber grinned mischievously. "Sure."

"Are you comfortable, Daddy?" Adrianna asked as she propped up her father, Howard Mitchell, against the pillows in the Victorian master bedroom he'd once shared with her mother, Vanessa, before she'd succumbed to breast cancer two years ago.

"I am. Thank you, baby girl." Her father patted her hand. "For coming back home. I really missed you."

"And I missed you, too," Adrianna replied. She'd only been back a few weeks, but she was glad she'd come.

Gone was the distinguished, poised governor with the salt-and-pepper hair who could simply will something and it was done. In his place was a weak man with thinning hair and a quiet whisper of a voice who depended on her or his nurses to take care of him. Her father had been diagnosed with colon cancer. He was gravely ill and the disease had taken its toll, so much so it appeared he'd become old practically overnight. Adrianna knew how much it must be hurting her father to have to depend on others for his well-being.

Even though she'd made a name for herself in the

culinary scene as a reviewer for *Foodies* magazine under the pseudonym Riley Ward, Adrianna had come rushing home as soon as her ex-husband, Phillip, had confided in her just how ill her father was. She'd thought his cancer was in remission, but apparently it had come back full steam. And so she'd packed up and left behind her condo in Chicago and moved in with her father at the family mansion in the Hamptons.

Foodies, on the other hand, was happy to finally have her stationed closer to the corporate office in New York instead of sending her articles. Now that she was back in her hometown, she had the desire to get back into cooking. Reviewing was great, but cooking was her true passion. She'd heard through the grapevine that Lawrence Enterprises, the Goliath of multimedia empires, might be interested in starting a food show on one of their networks and she hoped to throw her hat in the ring.

"You know Phillip came by the other day," her father said.

"Oh yeah?" Adrianna rolled her eyes upward. Why would he think that information was relevant? Did he think she'd forgotten the real reason she'd married Phillip Wright in the first place? It was because of her father. She'd married Phillip to save his good reputation so he could run for governor again. The fact that she loved and was pregnant with another man's baby was inconsequential.

Marry Phillip or else I will disinherit you and you will be left penniless to take care of your bastard child.

Those words still rang in Adrianna's mind as if he'd just spoken them to her. Her dying father was the reason why she'd lost the one man she'd ever truly loved: Dante Moore.

"Let's not talk about this now, Daddy," Adrianna

replied, sitting down in the chair by his bedside and taking his hand in hers. It was amazing how frail he was given how larger-than-life he once was. She remembered cowering to his six-foot presence as a child and now here he was bedridden.

"Why did you never give Phillip the chance?" her father questioned. "He could have made you happy."

"Daddy, must we get into this now?" Adrianna replied. She'd barely been back a few weeks and he was already bringing up a sore subject.

"You know how much Phillip loved you. Hell, still does. It's not too late if you want to make things right."

"Make things right, Daddy?" Adrianna rose from his bed and walked over to the window to look out over the courtyard. The overcast sky reflected how she felt. "Things were wrong the moment you threatened to cut me off if I didn't. They were wrong because I didn't love Phillip. I never did and I never will."

"How can you know that? You never gave the marriage a chance."

"After I lost the baby, there was no reason to go on with the marriage," Adrianna returned tersely. "I'd lost the best part of me and there was no reason to continue living a farce, but I did, Daddy. I continued for three long years until you got reelected and he won the congressional seat—or did you forget that fact?"

"No, I haven't forgotten what you did for me then or now. I'm just grateful to have you home, baby girl. This house has been empty since your mama passed."

Adrianna felt guilty. That was the last time she'd been home for any significant period of time to see her father, which was nearly two years ago. She'd never truly forgiven him for his betrayal. She hadn't been able to help him grieve the loss of her dear mother, probably because she felt as if she'd been living in her own private hell for years—unable to move forward, yet unable to go back, to claim a life, a love, that was denied her.

Adrianna swiftly turned around. "I know. It's why I'm here now, Daddy. Get some rest and I'll be back later." She strode to the door and closed it behind her. She was walking down the hall when she collided with her cousin Madison Mitchell.

"Ohmigod! You scared the bejesus out of me," Adrianna commented, clutching her chest.

Up until she'd moved to Chicago, Madison had been more of a sister to Adrianna than a cousin. From the time she'd been six until she'd turned twenty, they had confided all their deepest, darkest secrets to each other. Yet they couldn't be more different. Adrianna was much more reserved than free-spirited Madison. Adrianna guessed that was why being a publicity agent suited Madison. She could go with the flow. If anyone had been expected to get pregnant at twenty, it would have been Madison, not Adrianna. She could still remember the look of absolute horror on her father's face when he'd discovered she was pregnant.

"Sorry, cuz, I'd heard you were back in town and wanted to see how you were doing. Coming back to the scene of the crime after all these years couldn't have been easy."

Adrianna rolled her eyes upward. "Thanks for the reminder, Maddie."

"Well, you haven't lived in New York in nearly a decade so it would stand to reason you might be apprehensive about coming home."

"Well, I'm not," Adrianna replied, not looking her in the eye and stalking down the hall to her bedroom where somehow her bags had been miraculously unpacked.

She was sure she could thank their butler, Nigel, for unpacking her belongings.

"You sure about that?" Madison asked, plopping down on her bed.

"Yes," Adrianna said confidently. "You are looking well." She eyed her cousin's flamboyant blond hair, which she was sure had some weave in it, big hoop earrings, bright-colored kimono and knee-high boots. She was every bit the New York fashionista and made Adrianna feel dowdy in comparison, wearing black slacks and a pink-and-black sweater.

"Thank you, doll. So, catch me up. What are your plans while you're here in town?"

"Well, for starters I intend to reclaim my life," Adrianna replied. "I want to get back into cooking again and there might be an opportunity at Lawrence Enterprises."

"Sounds promising," Madison said, "though I have to tell you Ian Lawrence is no longer available. His attorney snapped him up and he's head over heels."

"I'm not interested in him in a private capacity, only a professional one," Adrianna returned. "I hear he's going to start a new food show on his network."

Madison chuckled. "I never did understand your fascination with getting your hands dirty, especially when you could afford a chef, but to each his own. Is work the reason you're back?"

"I'm here for Father. In case you hadn't noticed, he's dying."

"Is that the only reason?" Madison searched her cousin's eyes for some semblance of the truth, but saw none.

"Yes."

"Really?" Madison raised an eyebrow. "Because I

enjoyed your glowing review of Renaissance, Dante Moore's new restaurant in Harlem. Matter of fact, I can't wait to eat there."

"Madison, don't go there!"

"What?" Madison asked innocently, even though she knew that saying Dante Moore's name out loud was sacrilege in this house.

"I said I don't want you to go there, so drop it."

"Fine," Madison returned. "If you want to continue to bury the name of your first love, then fine. It's your life."

"Yes, it is. And Dante Moore is no longer a part of it."

Dante put the finishing touches on the gourmet basket he was making to bring to *Foodies* magazine on Monday afternoon. He owed Riley Ward for the wonderful review and Dante intended on bringing this token of his appreciation for the man to enjoy for lunch.

"Wow! You've put together quite a lunch," his sous-chef, Marvin Diaz, stated as he quartered several quails in preparation for the special on tonight's menu.

"Renaissance wouldn't be on the map if we hadn't gotten that great review." Dante added some truffle sauce over his roasted duck which included a savory bread pudding.

When he was finished, he packed the tinfoil containers into a basket along with a bottle of his best white wine and headed to *Foodies,* located in midtown Manhattan.

The *Foodies* corporate office was a bustling hub of activity. As soon as Dante stepped through the doors, his nose instantly smelled sautéed garlic and fresh basil wafting through the air. Someone was cooking something good, perhaps for the cover?

Confidently, he strode to the reception desk. "Dante Moore here to see Riley Ward."

"Do you have an appointment?" the receptionist, an older woman with a perfectly coiffed chignon asked.

"No, but I brought goodies." Dante held up the woven basket.

The woman eyed it suspiciously at first, but then the aroma must have wafted through the basket because she commented, "That does smell good. But I'm sorry, our reviewers must remain impartial."

Dante's brows furrowed in a frown. He had come there with a purpose in mind, to show his gratitude to the man who had jump-started his new restaurant, and he had no intention of allowing the receptionist to deter him from speaking his mind. A courier approached the desk at just that moment, distracting her with the delivery of several large packages. Dante saw an opportunity and slid past him and into the interior offices. Dante glanced at the plaques outside each doorway until he came to Riley Ward's. The door was closed, so he knocked.

"Come in," a voice said from the other side.

Dante twisted the door knob and burst into the room with his basket of gourmet entrees and a large smile. Then he saw the inhabitant of the room.

"Adrianna?" Dante took in her round face, petite nose, big almond-shaped brown eyes, high exotic cheekbones and pink-tinted lips. Although her hair was longer than he remembered and hung in luxurious big waves down her shoulders and she was dressed maturely in a red streamlined sheath dress with cap sleeves, she still looked like the girl he'd fallen in love with all those years ago at culinary school.

He'd been so full of hope and promise for the future back then. After several odd jobs, he'd finally realized his talent lay in cooking, and he dedicated himself to the craft. Although he was in his mid-twenties and Adrianna had been so young and innocent, barely twenty when they'd met, the year they'd spent together had been the best year of his life and one he'd never forgotten.

"Dante!" Adrianna's heart nearly leaped out of her chest. Coming face-to-face with the man she'd dreamed of for nearly a decade was startling. He was just as handsome, but much more muscular with a broad chest and ripped arms. The Dante she remembered was slim and clean-cut, not this edgy creature standing in front of her with a close-cropped haircut and goatee, who wore Armani and Ferragamo shoes and smelled woodsy. The Dante in front of her now was all man and looked like he had just stepped off the runway.

For a moment the last decade washed away and all Dante could do was stare into Adrianna's eyes as images of the two of them cooking and sampling each other's food and bodies crossed his mind, images of the two of them picnicking in Central Park or ice skating at Rockefeller Center washed over him. Then, just as swiftly they all came to a screeching halt as the memory of him coming to the apartment she'd shared with her cousin Madison and learning that she'd eloped with another man came to mind. That's when he said, "What the *hell* are you doing here?"

Chapter 2

"Excuse me?" Suddenly Adrianna snapped out of her reverie as if she'd been slapped. "I could ask you the same thing. You did just burst into *my* office."

Dante stepped back to take another glance at the plaque on the wall outside the door. It read Riley Ward.

"The plaque out there says Riley Ward," Dante returned, turning the full force of his anger directly at her, "not Adrianna Wright."

"Riley Ward is the pseudonym I use."

"Why the cloak-and-dagger?" Dante shut the door and placed the picnic basket on the coffee table near her desk. "Why not write under your real name? Or did you do this on purpose so I wouldn't know who you really were?" His voice was cool and disapproving.

"For your information, I didn't want anyone to think I was using my name and influence as a way to get ahead in the business. I wanted to stand on my own two feet."

She didn't want to use the prestige of her father being governor of New York to sway anyone to hire her.

"Oh, really? That didn't seem to matter much to you when you ran away a decade ago to marry someone more acceptable. You were all about name and prestige."

"You don't know what you're talking about," Adrianna returned.

"Why don't you enlighten me?" Dante had been dying to know the answer to that question for ten years and it was high time he got some answers. "Because I swore it was to marry another man even though you were spending your days and nights making love with me."

Adrianna started to speak, but then realized she didn't have a smart comeback. She couldn't tell Dante the real reason she'd left Manhattan, which was that she'd been carrying his child.

Dante smirked as he walked toward her. "What? No witty retort?"

Adrianna stepped backward until her bottom was pinned against the desk. There was something dangerous about this version of Dante and she admitted she was both nervous and excited by it. His eyes were unfathomable, yet she couldn't resist staring into them. As he approached, Adrianna's stomach began to flutter uncontrollably and she blinked several times to stop herself from acting like a silly schoolgirl, but she couldn't. Dante was getting to her just as he had when she was twenty years old, except this time she was supposed to be a sophisticated divorcée, not a girl. No such luck!

When he finally came to stand mere inches from her, Adrianna thought—no, *hoped*—he would kiss her. She'd missed the touch, the feel of those warm, full lips on hers and the swirling, dizzying, mind-blowing emotion Dante could evoke from her. She'd never felt that way when her ex-husband, Phillip, kissed her. Instead Phillip's kisses had merely been bearable. But Dante was a whole other story.

Dante looked intently into Adrianna's face, saw the longing in those brown depths and was close to giving in to temptation. How easy it would be to relive the past and just live in the moment, taking all she had to give. But his pride wouldn't let him. Adrianna had made a fool of him once and he wasn't about to let her do it again.

He caressed her cheek and leaned down until his lips were near hers. Adrianna's back arched as she waited for him to plant one on her, but instead he said, "I know you want me to kiss you, but you know what? I'm not going to give you the satisfaction. I'm not your boy toy that you can use for a while then when you're done toss aside for someone more acceptable."

His head popped up just as Adrianna's hand came toward his face and he escaped a smack to the jaw. "Ah, so there is still a spitfire in there and not some poised society wife." He'd seen society photos of her and her ex-husband in the newspapers and magazines. She'd completely altered herself to fit a certain image. He hadn't been surprised when he'd heard of the marriage's demise because she wasn't being herself.

"Damn you, Dante!" Adrianna said, straightening and walking toward the window. He'd gotten to her and he knew it. It was evident she was longing for his kiss and she was irked by her body's response to him after all this time. She'd thought if she ever saw him again that he would have no effect. Clearly, she'd been wrong.

"No, damn you, Adrianna," Dante replied. "So what I played with you just then. It's no more than what you did to me ten years ago. You played with my heart and then you tossed it aside like a ragdoll."

"I never meant to hurt you."

"You made me believe that you loved me, only to find out you never really loved me at all. And to find out from your cousin of all people? My God, you didn't even have the guts to tell me to my face. You were a coward!"

"I'm sorry about that, Dante, truly I am." Adrianna turned away and faced the window. Afraid he'd see the tears forming in her eyes. He had deserved to hear the words from her, but at the time she'd been afraid to for fear she wouldn't be able to go through with her father's orders and Dante would see the truth in her eyes.

"Sorry? Sorry?" he yelled, coming toward her. "You snuck off like a lying, deceitful, two-timing harlot. What were you doing with me, Adrianna? Slumming? You couldn't get your thrills from Boy Wonder so you had to go slumming in the hood with the poor orphan?"

"No!" Adrianna spun on her heel at the hurtful words coming out of Dante's mouth. She knew she deserved them after the horrible way she'd treated him, but they were still hard to hear. "That's not true. I loved you, Dante."

"So now we get to the truth." Dante's eyes grew wide as he spoke. "You loved me, just not enough, right? I didn't come with all the trappings of wealth like Phillip. I was just some poor struggling sous-chef, not an upcoming congressman being groomed into politics. I had nothing to offer you back then. And you were accustomed to a certain lifestyle. Or so your father told me when I confronted him."

"You confronted him?" Why had her father never told her?

"Yes, because I just couldn't believe that the woman I loved would treat me that way."

"I'm sorry, Dante. I had no idea."

"Your father had no problem filling me in on exactly who you were. He explained that you never truly loved me and that you were taking up with me, just to get back at him. It was teenage rebellion, he'd called it. And since I was older, I should be able to understand, a child getting back at their parents. But you know what, Adrianna? I didn't understand it one damn bit."

Tears sprung to Adrianna's eyes. "Dante, you are so wrong."

"You know, Adrianna, I don't see you giving me another explanation, but what I don't get is why come back at all? Why give my restaurant a glowing review? Why not give the review to someone else?"

"You're right. I could have given your review to another reviewer, but I didn't want to. I felt I owed it to you."

"So you didn't think my food was great?" Dante's temper rose slightly. Now, he was insulted. "You just felt guilty. Were you lying in the review?"

Adrianna shook her head vehemently. "Of course not. I would never compromise my reputation. The food at your restaurant and the service was impeccable. I tasted it myself. That's why you got a good review, nothing more."

Adrianna had come to his restaurant? When? Why hadn't he seen her? It was hard to believe she would have ever gotten past him. Had she been in disguise? "And you're back now? Why?"

Adrianna's head hung low. "My father is ill. Cancer."

"I'm sorry to hear that," Dante responded softly. Howard Wright was not one of his favorite people. He remembered the first time they'd met. He'd come bursting into the restaurant Dante had been working in at the time, demanding that Dante end the affair with his daughter. He'd been quite insistent that Adrianna was better off with Phillip Wright, a man more suited to someone of her class and education, but Dante had said he wouldn't give her up. He had no idea that six months later Adrianna would betray him. Despite that, Dante didn't wish illness on the man.

"Well, you've said your piece, so why are you here, Dante?"

"Why am I here? Hmm, let me see," Dante replied sarcastically. "I thought I'd come by and thank my benefactor for the wonderful review by bringing a sample of some of the new items on my menu." He nodded to the picnic basket. "But then again I had no idea who Riley Ward truly was."

"And now that you do?"

"I'm sorry I came," Dante responded. "I should have left well enough alone because I don't know the woman standing before me." Dante strode to the exit, but then stopped at the doorway. "But I guess I never did. Enjoy the food."

Seconds later, he was gone. Adrianna's shoulders sagged and she plopped down in her leather ergonomic chair. She had expected anger, but the unmistakable look of disgust and disappointment in Dante's eyes destroyed her equilibrium.

Her mind flashed back to ten years ago, when she'd discovered she was pregnant. She'd been so scared that the only person she'd confided in was Madison. Who would have known that her father's aide was having her followed and had relayed that she'd gone to a Planned Parenthood clinic? Apparently, her father had been concerned about negative publicity in light of his reelection as governor and had her followed. She'd been furious when he'd confronted her about her reasons for going there and had adamantly refused to tell him why. But Howard Wright was not to be trifled with, and in front of her mother, Vanessa, he'd demanded the truth. She'd had no choice but to reveal she was six weeks pregnant.

Her mother had been understanding. She'd made a mistake because she was young and in love. Her father, on the other hand, hadn't been so tolerant. He'd berated her irresponsibility for getting pregnant and how it could ruin her life, but the real truth was he was more concerned with how it would ruin his chances of reelection. Being a Republican and having a pregnant, unmarried daughter was career suicide at the time.

"I love Dante," Adrianna had said, "and we'll make this work."

"How?" Howard Wright had asked. "That young man is just beginning his culinary career and you want to saddle him with a wife and child."

And marry they would have because Dante wouldn't have settled for anything less, but her father's words had given her pause. Perhaps he was right. Was Dante ready to be a father?

"Marry Phillip Wright. He'll be a good husband and father and give your child a stable home."

"No." Adrianna had shaken her head. "I don't love Phillip. You know I love Dante. Why won't you listen to me?" He'd tried to throw his protégé Phillip Wright at her the year before, but Adrianna had resisted. She didn't want to be a politician's wife. She'd seen her mother and despite the love between her parents, she'd known it had made their lives difficult, constantly being under public scrutiny.

"Do what's right," her father had said. "Don't be selfish. Think about what's best for your child."

Adrianna had turned to her mother for comfort, but she was sobbing into her handkerchief.

"I am doing what's right. Dante has a right to know he's going to be a father and I'm going to tell him." Adrianna had headed toward the door and that's when her father had delivered the ultimate blow.

"If you tell Dante and marry him, I'm cutting you off," he'd said. "You will be penniless, without a dime to your name."

"You would do that? You would disinherit me?" The money and family business wasn't even his, it was her mother's. Without it, he would never have gotten elected.

"Mom, are you going to let him do this?" She looked to her mother for assistance, but instead she'd bowed down to her father's will.

"If that's what it takes." Her father's voice had been resolute when he'd spoken. "Listen, girl, I am protecting you and this entire family."

Ten years ago, she'd been weak and spineless and caved in to her father's demands. "Fine. I will do it," she'd said, "but know this. I love Dante and nothing you say or do is ever going to change that." Now look at her. She was a divorced thirty-one-year-old.

What had she done? Why hadn't she had the courage to stand up to her father and fight for the man she loved and the life they deserved? So what if her father had cut off her trust fund. At least they would have had each other. Perhaps their child would have made it. Had she lost the baby as punishment for her lies and sin? Adrianna wondered. If Dante ever found out that she'd been pregnant and lost their child, he would never forgive her. The moment she'd decided to keep the truth from him, their happily ever after was gone forever.

* * *

Adrianna Wright was back in Manhattan and as strikingly beautiful as the last time he'd seen her, perhaps more so.

How could this be? Dante wondered as he walked out of *Foodies* magazine headquarters in a daze. How could the one woman he'd ever loved, the woman he'd never truly gotten over, suddenly bounce back into his life as if she'd never left?

He didn't find the answer as his driver took him to the Harlem Community Center where Malik was sure to be working late.

Dante leaned back and rested his head against the leather cushion. He closed his eyes in an attempt to relax. Malik lived and breathed the community center which is why the Children's Aid Network had put him in charge of several centers throughout Manhattan. Due to both restaurants' success, Dante had foregone the headache of driving in favor of having a chauffeur.

The drive to HCC from midtown Manhattan was nearly an hour long due to traffic and gave Dante too much time to think about Adrianna and how beautiful she looked. Time had been good to her. She wasn't as slim as she'd been as a young girl. Instead, her shape had become more womanly, and had filled out with full breasts and delicious curves. Curves that Dante would love to run his hand down.

Damn her! He shouldn't even be having these thoughts after the shabby way she'd treated him ten years ago, but then again his libido had always been in overdrive around her. Quentin and Malik had thought she'd been too young for him back then as he was five years her senior, but he couldn't resist her charms. And now she was back. What was he supposed to do? How was he supposed to feel?

She'd devastated him ten years ago by walking away from him. He'd never understood or figured out how or why the woman he'd adored could abandon him so easily for another man. Or that an affair could have been going on under his nose the entire time. It was certainly how her father had presented the facts. She was a young girl sowing her wild oats before marrying someone more appropriate. Dante had felt duped by the wealthy socialite. He'd felt like a fool. He'd tried to have long-term relationships after Adrianna, but the truth of the matter was she'd broken him for any other woman.

Her leaving and subsequent refusal to give him any type of closure had tapped into the abandonment issues he'd faced by having his own mother leave him when he was just a toddler. And even now, he still didn't understand. She'd offered him no real reasons for why she'd done what she'd done. Only that she was sorry. What good did that do him?

The jolt of the car stopping brought Dante back to reality and he stepped out into the cool spring air. He walked past the reception area renovated nearly two years ago and headed straight to Malik's office.

He waved at Malik's assistant and right hand, Theresa, before walking into his office. Malik had an open door policy and Dante doubted he would mind.

"What's up?" Malik asked when Dante unceremoniously walked into his office and collapsed into the chair opposite him.

"You will not believe who rose from the ashes," Dante replied.

Malik knew such things were possible as his own stepfather had emerged after twenty-five years, but thankfully he'd had Peyton to help him deal with it. "I've no idea. Who is it?"

"None other than my duplicitous ex-girlfriend, Adrianna Wright!"

"You're kidding, right?" Malik sat straight up in his chair. "Where has she been all these years?"

Dante shrugged. "Who knows? And who cares? The problem is she is here now and has been writing under the pseudonym Riley Ward."

"Adrianna gave you the glowing review?"

"Yep."

"Wow!" Malik paused and rubbed his perpetual five o'clock shadow. "Why now? Why come back?"

"Apparently, her father is dying of cancer, so she's come back to New York to take care of him."

"And figured she'd toss you a bone?"

"Something like that."

"Did she have anything to say for herself after all this time?"

"Like what!" Dante jumped out of the chair, knocking it to the floor. "What could she possibly say, Malik, that would matter now? Apologize? Hell, that won't make up for her leaving me for another man. It's not like she can take it all back."

"No, she can't." Malik walked over from his desk and picked up the chair. "It's just hard to believe she's back after all these years and is the mysterious reviewer that sang your praises."

"You're telling me," Dante replied, folding his arms across his chest and leaning against the wall. "I hate owing her anything."

"You owe her nothing," Malik stated, looking Dante dead in the eye. "If anything, she owes you for the horrible way she treated you. Because of her you swore off women."

"I haven't sworn off women."

"No? I disagree. You haven't had a serious relationship since Adrianna."

"That's not true…" Dante started, but then paused when he realized Malik was right. He hadn't had a committed relationship in the past ten years, at least not one that lasted longer than a few months. "Okay, I guess you're right."

"I know I am. That chick did a number on you and you never recovered."

"Well, what do I do now?" Despite how angry with her he was, he still felt vulnerable to Adrianna's charms. The almost kiss in her office proved that.

"Don't let her do it to you a second time," Malik advised.

Dante laughed to himself. That was easier said than done.

Chapter 3

Dante was excited as he sat in the reception area on the tenth floor of Lawrence Enterprises late Wednesday morning. He'd arrived for the meeting Ian had set up with his head of development for a new food show on his network, WTTG. Despite the whirl of emotions going through his mind about Adrianna resurfacing in Manhattan after ten years, he was eager to get started on the next phase of his career. He'd seen what having one's own food show could do for a chef's career. Look at the Emerils, Rachael Rays, Bobby Flays and Paula Deens of the world. They'd started out on television, but were now a brand from talk shows to cookbooks to kitchen products. They were raking in the endorsements.

A few moments later, Ian walked toward him with a tall, blond gentleman in a silver designer suit. "Dante, I'd like you to meet Todd Allen. He's the President of Programming and Production here at WTTG."

"Pleasure to meet you." Todd extended his hand and Dante gave it a hearty shake. "I've heard nothing but great things about your food and talent in the kitchen. Let's see if we can turn that into magic on screen."

"Sounds good to me," Dante said. Todd looked like an affable person so hopefully the interview would be a breeze.

"I will leave you both to talk," Ian replied, "as I have another engagement. I look forward to hearing what you both come up with."

"Follow me." Todd led Dante into a nearby conference room and closed the door. "So, Dante, what is your culinary point of view?"

"Well, my culinary point of view is New American cuisine with soul food and Spanish flairs."

"Have you given any thought to what point of view you would bring to the television show?"

"Actually, I have," Dante returned. "Ian may have told you but I've broadened my horizons to include catering and I handle our family dinners every Sunday. So I think some type of entertaining show would be in order. I don't know my exact ethnic background, but I've always been drawn to those flavors."

"You would certainly have a unique show—New American/soul food cooking with a Latin twist." Todd rubbed his jaw. "So have you ever been inside a television kitchen studio?"

"I've been inside many kitchens."

"Oh, but a television kitchen is much different." Todd rose from his chair and walked toward the door. "Follow me."

Dante was curious as he followed Todd through a series of hallways until finally pushing open two double doors and stepping into an enormous television studio complete with a mock kitchen.

"Wow! Lawrence Enterprises certainly didn't waste any time setting up a kitchen," Dante commented. "A few minutes ago, Ian led me to believe this was something he'd come up with off the cuff."

"We've been tossing the idea back and forth for a while now, but as soon as Ian says he wants something, we make it happen."

Dante's smile widened in approval. Why wasn't he surprised? A multimillionaire need only snap his fingers and people would jump. He stepped over the plethora of cords and walked around the cameras to the kitchen counter. He paused for a moment to look around. He could definitely see himself in front of the camera.

"If you don't mind, I'd like to take some test footage of you," Todd said.

"Right now?"

"No better time than the present to see if you have what it takes."

Before Dante knew what was happening, technicians were rushing inside the room and setting up while a makeup artist came over to pat his face with some foundation and powder. Dante frowned.

"Don't worry. Real men do wear makeup and you'll need it for the camera," Todd replied.

The rest of the taping went so fast, Dante would have sworn he dreamed it. There was a script for cooking one of his famous recipes from Dante's. How had Ian gotten his hands on that? A certain petite lawyer came to mind. Trust Sage to stick her nose where it didn't belong.

There were so many things to learn from blocking and knowing exactly where he needed to be, to which camera he had to look at. Camera one would film him while camera two would focus on what he was cooking on the gas stove. And of course, there was the teleprompter. Dante thought he would have trouble following the script on the teleprompter, while cooking and communicating with the viewers about what he was creating as he gave cooking tips and shared tidbits of his life. A lot was required of him, but Dante thrived on another challenge in his burgeoning career.

After he'd finished taping, Todd commented on what a great job he'd done, so Dante was feeling pretty sure of himself until he headed out of the studio past reception and a familiar face caught his eye. Surely, it couldn't be her again! But just as his heart had beaten a hundred times a minute in her office the other day, it did again now. Except this time, he thought it would leap out of his chest.

Before he could speak, Adrianna must have sensed his presence and glanced up. "Dante? What are you doing here?"

"I could ask you the same question," he returned, purposely not answering her. Instead, his eyes were scanning every feature on her face, from her expressive brown eyes to her ruby-red lipstick. She was definitely out to impress if the tailored red suit jacket and short skirt were any indication. If she'd dressed to show she was in control, she'd done it, as the vibrant red color suited her coloring perfectly.

Adrianna sighed. She was in no mood for a confrontation with Dante, especially not before her big meeting which would decide whether she remained a reviewer or branched back out into cooking. "Do we have to do this again?" She needed to stay focused and positive. She hadn't cooked professionally in years and needed to convince the folks at Lawrence Enterprises that despite her background she had something truly special to offer if given her own show. It was a long shot, she knew, but she had to give it a try.

"Are you trying to ingratiate yourself into every aspect of my life?" Dante queried. "How else can you explain why you're here?"

"For your information, I'm here looking into a position as the host of LE's newest cooking show."

"Excuse me?" Ian hadn't told him that he was considering any other potential hosts. He'd thought he was a shoo-in, but apparently not.

"Yes, a friend of mine put in a good word for me with the higher-ups so I think I have a good shot at the job."

Dante's face split into a grin. "Oh, you think so?" Adrianna clearly hadn't lost her confidence. It reminded him of when she'd told him she was the better chef all those years ago.

"Well, yes, of course," Adrianna responded, a little perturbed at his attitude. "I know great food and although I may be a reviewer I haven't lost my zest for cooking. And I'm sure I can portray that to viewers."

"Good luck." Dante chuckled.

"Do you really mean that or are you just being facetious?"

"I meant may the best man or woman win," Dante added.

Adrianna's brow crinkled into a frown. "What is that supposed to mean?"

"It means that I am also up for the host position. You know, a chef with real experience cooking in a kitchen day in and day out as opposed to a novice such as yourself."

"A novice? I am no such thing. I went to culinary school like you and trained at Le Cordon Bleu."

Dante chuckled again. "When? In between dinner parties? Isn't that what socialites like yourself do when they're bored?"

"You arrogant son of a—" Adrianna was about to say something brash, but the receptionist had looked up, interested in their intense conversation. So Adrianna stepped farther away, out of her earshot.

"If I recall correctly, you did write that I was the best new chef in New York, right?"

Adrianna's eyes narrowed. "I did, but a little healthy competition will help knock you down off that pedestal."

"I've no worries," Dante replied. "I have an ace in the hole."

"And what's that?"

"Sage's boyfriend, Ian Lawrence."

Adrianna's face immediately became crestfallen. "Sage? Your…your friend Sage's boyfriend is Ian Lawrence."

"One and the same."

Adrianna glanced toward the door and her stomach began to sink. "So you think my going in there is a moot point?"

Dante shrugged. "Some would say yes."

"Well, the fat lady hasn't sung yet." Adrianna walked toward him and pulled on his tie. "Hold your horses, Dante Moore, because you've got competition and I'm not going quietly into the night."

"That's a shame because that is your motto, isn't it?"

Todd Allen walked through the double doors at that exact moment. Dante could see he was clearly taken aback at seeing his two candidates sizing each other up, but just as quickly he recovered. "Ms. Wright, it's good to see you. Looks like you've met Dante Moore. He's a restaurateur in town."

Adrianna glanced behind her shoulder at Dante. "Yes, I am familiar with Mr. Moore."

Dante chuckled to himself. She was more than just familiar with him. She was acquainted with every part of his body.

"I'm eager to speak with you," Todd commented. "Please follow me. I'd love to hear what you have to say. Dante, it was great meeting you."

"Likewise."

After they'd left, Dante stewed and paced the floors of LE's lobby. He wanted to strangle Ian for presenting this hosting gig as if it was a done deal when that was far from the case. He pulled his cell phone from his pocket and dialed Sage to tell her about her beloved.

"So what kind of game is your boyfriend playing?" Dante asked, cutting to the chase.

"Dante?" Sage asked from the other end of the line. "What's got you on fire?"

"I came to LE today to meet with Ian and his team about the cooking show."

"That was today? How did it go?"

"Well, apparently, Ian has other people in mind."

"What other people?" Sage's voice rose. "He didn't mention anything to me."

"Well, *he* does and it just so happens to be Adrianna Wright." Dante dropped the bombshell he'd kept to himself for several days.

"Adrianna!" Sage hadn't heard the name in years. "What rock did she crawl out from under?" Back in the day, Sage had thought Adrianna was perfect for Dante.

Because they were so close in age, they'd gotten along famously—until Adrianna broke Dante's heart into a thousand little pieces.

"From Chicago. Apparently, she's been holed up there for years and has finally come home to roost. She's up for the hosting job as well."

"Over my dead body!" Sage would not let the lying, deceitful woman hurt Dante again and take a golden opportunity away from him.

"Sage, I don't want you to get involved," Dante responded.

"Then why tell me?" Sage was furious with Ian for leading Dante on.

"Because…I just needed to know if you knew about this competition and clearly you didn't know anything about it."

"Of course I didn't," Sage returned. "If I had, I would have given you a heads-up, not left you flying blind."

Dante sighed. "I know. But if Ian doesn't think I'm the right man for this job, then I don't want it."

"Dante, don't talk that way. This show would be the perfect outlet for you to move to the next level in your career. You're a star and it's just a matter of time before everyone else knows it."

Sage knew how to stroke his ego. "Thanks, Sage. I don't want you to think I'm walking away because I'm not. I just want it to be a fair fight and if you put yourself in the middle it won't be."

"You'd better not walk away. You're ten times the chef that woman will ever be. So, you don't want me to speak with Ian on your behalf?"

"No, and if you do and I find out, I'll be really upset with you. I need to get this hosting gig on my own merit and because Ian and his team think I am the best chef for the job."

Sage responded, "If that's how you want to play this, I'll do as you ask, but how are *you?* Seeing Adrianna after all these years must have come as quite a shock."

Dante remained silent for several minutes.

"Dante?"

"Well, I've known she was back for several days. She is the elusive Riley Ward."

"You've got to be kidding. So, not only does she lie in her personal life, she lies in her career, too."

"There's nothing wrong with using a pseudonym." Dante was surprised he was even defending Adrianna.

"Not if you're Adrianna Wright." Sage paused for a few moments, then returned to the phone conversation. "Listen, Dante. I have to go, but I will call you later."

"Okay, talk to you soon." Dante closed his phone. He had no doubt that Sage would give him an earful later about him keeping the news that Adrianna was back to himself. He was about to head out, but his curiosity got the better of him and he stopped in his tracks. Glancing at the double doors, Dante wondered how Adrianna was doing. Despite her bravado, he could tell she was nervous about applying for the host position. He'd had a long thriving culinary career while she had been hiding behind a pen. Or maybe he was voicing his own insecurities. Maybe she was in there knocking it out of the ballpark.

Adrianna was frustrated as Todd led her back to reception. She'd been all confidence with Dante about her capabilities as a chef. Problem was she had no idea that she'd be expected to do a pilot taping today. She'd thought this was an informal sit-down meeting to discuss ideas about the show. Surprise! She'd had to remove her jacket and cook in her new red Dior suit! She wasn't prepared to be pushed in front of a camera so quickly. She'd stumbled half a dozen times over the script. The thought that Todd Allen would believe she was host material quickly went up in smoke when she'd missed adding several ingredients while cooking her truffle macaroni and cheese—her signature dish!

If this was any indication of her own show's success, she would be a total disaster. She'd failed to jump-start her career.

"Thank you so much for coming in, Ms. Wright." Todd sounded gracious as he escorted her out even though she knew she'd failed to deliver.

Adrianna accepted his handshake. "Thank you for the opportunity, Mr. Allen."

Adrianna exited the double doors with her head hung low. This was a devastating blow to her self-esteem. What she could use was a bubble bath and a stiff drink and not necessarily in that order. She was surprised when Dante put down the magazine he'd been perusing to rise from the sofa in the lobby.

"You're still here?" Adrianna asked.

"Guess so."

"Why?" Her mind was spinning with bewilderment.

Dante shrugged. "I don't know." And that was truth. He didn't know why he'd stayed. Why should he care about her audition, especially when it had the potential to hurt his own chances?

Adrianna searched Dante's face, looking into his beautiful light brown eyes, eyes she used to get lost in. Was he concerned for her? Were there still feelings there after all these years and after everything she'd done to him? "You didn't have to, but thank you."

Dante grinned briefly with no trace of his former

animosity. It was the first civil moment they'd had since he'd burst into her offices at *Foodies* magazine. "So, where are you off to?" Dante asked as they both headed for the elevators.

"A cocktail," Adrianna answered honestly.

Dante checked his watch and it read three o'clock. "That bad, huh?"

Adrianna laughed derisively. "Join me and I'll tell you all about it."

Dante's first inclination was to say no and run for the hills. Adrianna couldn't be trusted, but she looked so very disappointed that he said, "Why not? I'm free."

Butterflies instantly somersaulted in Adrianna's belly at the thought of spending time alone with Dante. It had been over a decade since they'd been together, yet she found herself extremely conscious of his virile appeal.

They walked out of the Lawrence Enterprises tower and once outside, Dante took the lead. "Follow me. There's a great little place down the street that Sage and I have frequented a few times."

"Lead the way." Adrianna motioned for him to precede her.

The bar was empty since it wasn't quite happy hour yet, so Dante and Adrianna easily found a seat. As she hopped onto a stool, her nose caught a tantalizing whiff of Dante's aftershave. It was a crisp, citrusy scent, yet robust and masculine.

The bartender slid a bowl of nuts their way and asked, "What'll you have?"

"I'll have a vodka and cranberry," Adrianna replied.

"And I'll have a beer." Dante scooted his stool closer to Adrianna and turned to face her. "Since when did you start drinking hard liquor?" He remembered a certain evening that he'd had to put her to bed at the apartment she'd shared with Madison because she'd had one too many Long Island Iced Teas.

Adrianna tossed her silky mane of black luxurious curls to one side and Dante's stomach curled into a knot. He wanted to reach out and run his hands through it to remember the smell and the feel of it, but he stopped himself.

"Oh, I don't know," Adrianna replied as she removed her jacket. She was lying. She'd started on the strong stuff during her three-year marriage to Phillip. She'd been terribly unhappy and Phillip hadn't tried to connect with her. He'd been more concerned about his rising career. Like her father, he, too, had political aspirations. Add the fact that she was in love with another man and wanted a food career of her own and their marriage was doomed.

"You've certainly grown up," Dante commented as his eyes roved over her full breasts. He could see the round shape of them through the thin camisole and it made him want to mold them in his hands.

"Ah, yes, I have," Adrianna returned. She licked her lips to avoid appearing nervous because Dante's eyes weren't hooded now. She could see the appreciative male look in them as he gave her the once-over. "I'm not the naive nineteen-year-old girl that fell head over heels for you."

Dante cocked his head aside to glance at Adrianna. "I wouldn't have called you naive—more like sheltered."

The bartender returned with their cocktails and slid them across the counter. Just in time in Adrianna's opinion, because her mouth had gone dry with just one hungry look from Dante.

"Growing up in the public eye, I had to be. There couldn't be any scandals. We had to appear like we were the perfect family."

Although he had no idea what it was like to have a traditional family, he imagined it couldn't have been easy. "That had to be hard for you."

"It was. My every move was constantly being scrutinized. Who my friends were. Where I went. Who I dated."

"Who you married?" Dante inquired.

"Do you really want to go there?" Adrianna asked.

"No, I suppose not." Dante already knew the reason she'd married her ex-husband: Money and power. Back then, he'd had neither. "So tell me about your audition."

"Which part? The flubbed lines? Or the fact that I left out truffles in my signature macaroni dish?"

"Oh." Dante's mouth pursed into a frown.

"I had no idea I was expected to cook today. Otherwise, I wouldn't have worn this suit." Adrianna motioned down to her outfit.

"You look fabulous by the way."

"Thank you. The intent was to impress, not cook." Adrianna sipped her drink. "Of course, why didn't I think about that when I dressed this morning, that I was auditioning to host a cooking show?"

"Don't feel bad." Dante took a swig of his beer. "I wasn't thinking about it, either. So imagine my surprise when Todd led me into the studio to tape."

"So, how did you do?" When he went still, she asked, "You killed it, didn't you?" Her gaze lingered on his broad shoulders and athletic body and had no doubt he had.

Dante bunched his shoulders. "But it's no guarantee."

"You have Sage in your corner."

"And I asked her not intervene."

Dante was constantly surprising her today. "You did? Why would you do that?"

"I wanted it to be a fair fight. And it wouldn't be if Sage stepped in on my behalf. You deserved a shot at the job just as much as me." Dante took another swig of beer.

"But I haven't been slaving in the kitchen working my way up the top like you have."

"Ah, yes, the climb to the top hasn't been easy," Dante replied. "As you know I was sous-chef, but that didn't last long. After a few years, I became head chef and that's when the idea for my own restaurant began to take form."

"Tapas. That was unique," Adrianna responded, taking a drink of her cocktail.

"I'd always loved making small bites and amuse-bouches. Dante's allowed me the outlet. But trust me, it wasn't easy getting started. No one wanted to lend me money. I had no collateral and an untested theme. Quentin loaned me the money initially and once I paid him back, I took my profit and opened my next restaurant."

"You've done very well for yourself, Dante. You should be proud."

"I am. So what has Adrianna Wright been doing all these years?"

"Well, after my marriage ended, I went to Le Cordon Bleu in Paris. When I came back to the States, I tried to get back into cooking, but no one wanted to take a socialite-turned-chef seriously, so I began doing food reviews for a small Chicago magazine. Soon folks began to take notice and before I knew it, I was regarded as a knowledgeable source in the culinary industry."

"Not to downplay your accomplishments, but if you don't mind my asking, why didn't you come back to New

York? With a degree from Le Cordon Bleu in Paris, you could have gotten a job as a chef at any number of New York establishments."

"I don't know." Adrianna shrugged.

"Oh, I think you do." Dante looked deep into her eyes.

"Okay, you want honesty? I didn't want to come back and face my past."

"Face me?"

"I felt I didn't have the right to come back and disrupt your life after the unceremonious way I exited it."

"You're giving yourself a lot of credit that I was still pining away for you."

"Have you ever thought it was the other way around? Maybe I was still pining for you?" Adrianna locked gazes with Dante and for a long moment, the sexual tension that had been growing between them as they sat, grew.

Dante's pulse spiked. He was wound up as tight as a drum from the potent combination of Adrianna's nearness and the sexual draw of her lingering question. He wanted to take her back home and lose himself inside her, see if she still tasted as sweet, felt as good as silk on his skin, smelled warm and sweet like citrus and flowers all mixed together.

"Do you want to get out of here?" he suddenly asked, unable to control himself.

"Yes."

That one word was all Dante needed to hear as he closed out the bill with the bartender and helped her into his chauffeured town car. Once inside, his brain switched into overdrive as he lowered the privacy screen with one hand, and the other hand flew out around her neck to draw her face near. Her lips were incredibly soft against his as he pushed them apart to dive inside for a taste. She tasted like heaven and when her tongue tangled with his for supremacy, heat flooded his entire being. He pulled her close until they were chest to chest, belly to belly.

The kiss was so supercharged; it bombarded Adrianna with the pent-up desire of not having Dante's mouth on hers for ten years. Her body was humming with anticipation of what was to come. She'd longed for, waited for, wanted this moment and now that it was here, she intended to enjoy it fully.

She gripped his forearms as he slid his body directly over hers, his eyes conveying a deep desire. His tongue lavished hers with long, slow strokes until her belly knotted with tension and she began to ache between her thighs. She squirmed underneath him as she urged him on, eager to become one with him.

He obliged her by gripping her thighs and wrapping her legs around his waist. He pushed her skirt up around her waist. Her silky thighs quivered as his hands came in contact with her lacy underwear. He slipped his fingers beneath the satin and traced the slick folds of her feminine flesh. She was wet and ready for him. Dante couldn't wait to get her in his bed. He continued to stoke the flame. His tongue plunged deeper inside her mouth while his other hand found and molded one of her round breasts. Adrianna moaned aloud and Dante thought he would go insane if he didn't have her then.

Adrianna clutched his shoulders as Dante brought her to a fevered frenzy. The car stopped just as Adrianna was about to come. It left her feeling unfulfilled.

"Soon, baby, soon," Dante whispered as he lowered her skirt and sat up.

Dante pushed the intercom button for his chauffeur. "Johnny, give us a moment, please." Then he turned to

Adrianna. "Are you sure want this because now's the time for turning back."

Adrianna looked into the face of the man she'd once loved and said, "Yes, I want to make love to you."

"Then I promise to pleasure you until you're delirious," Dante said, as he jumped out of the car.

"Those are awful high expectations to live up to, Mr. Moore," Adrianna replied when Dante came around the other side to help her out.

"And I will live up to them." Dante grasped her hand and gently pulled her out of the vehicle.

Adrianna didn't see much of Dante's condo because as soon as the door shut, they flew into each other's arms.

They started in the hallway. Dante slung his jacket across the bedroom just before he backed her up against the door. Shivers ran through her body when he cupped her face, studied her features and dove his tongue inside her mouth. The kiss was heartfelt, deep and penetrating. It penetrated Adrianna's heart and awakened feelings and emotions she hadn't known still existed. She wrapped her arms around his broad, muscular shoulders. Their tongues mingled and mated as one complete unit, just as Adrianna remembered.

Dante twined his fingers through her curly tresses, burying his face before moving back to her cheeks and her full lips. He kissed her slow and deep, building the passion until every nerve sparked to life and every cell in Adrianna was ignited. He splayed his hands across her bottom and brought her into close contact with his engorged member.

Slowly he took liberties with other parts of her body. His hands traced the outline of her breasts underneath her jacket, stroked her nipples with the tips of his fingers.

Adrianna's breath caught in her throat, but didn't stop him from removing her jacket. Nor did she stop him when his hands reached behind her for the zipper on her skirt. Soon it was lying in a heap on the floor.

Dante lifted the camisole over Adrianna's head until all she was left wearing was her satin bra and panties. Adrianna had a beautiful body and Dante groaned deep in his throat. He wanted her completely naked.

"I want you so much," Dante murmured, his voice raw with need. He ripped open his shirt, sending buttons flying in every direction, and tossed it away.

"I want you, too," Adrianna whispered. She could see the deep longing in his gaze. She unzipped his pants and helped ease them down his muscular thighs, exposing a pair of sexy, black briefs, briefs that could do little to cover the hard length of his aroused member. He stepped out of his underwear and what she saw took her breath away. He was magnificent and so much more than she remembered. She reached out to caress his chest just as he unhooked the clasp at the front of the bra, freeing her firm breasts to his appreciative gaze. He massaged her breasts, caressing each dark nipple, until he finally lowered his head for a taste.

Adrianna moaned aloud when his mouth closed around each breast, branding it with his hot, wet tongue. She felt his hands move lower to the area between her thighs. He paused for a moment over her and he could feel her pulse quicken underneath his hand. He eased the panties down her thighs and before Adrianna could step out of them, he'd slid his finger inside her.

Dante found her wet with her own juices. He stroked her gently at first, then slowly began quickening the pace, bringing her to a fever pitch. Adrianna began making whimpering noises that told Dante she was enjoying what he was doing. Then he crouched to his knees to kiss the soft flesh of her inner thigh and then went farther to the apex at the center of her thighs. He teased it with his lips before penetrating the slick folds with his tongue. Adrianna shuddered and he knew he had her. He grabbed her hips and laved her womanly nub with slow and then fast flicks of his tongue.

"Oh yes, oh yes," Adrianna cried aloud, encouraging Dante on his quest as pleasure radiated through her core.

Dante rose quickly and reached for his pants. He always kept a condom, just in case. He quickly sheathed himself before returning to Adrianna. She was leaning weak-kneed against the door with a longing gaze and he intended to give her everything he had. He recaptured her lips, parting them with his tongue to invade her mouth. His hands tightened around her waist to bring her closer to him. He positioned himself, rubbing his member against her and Adrianna purred. She parted her legs and he grabbed her hips and dove inside her. Adrianna wrapped her legs around his waist as he began thrusting inside her. It felt so good and so sweet.

Delicious sensations took over Dante as he found a slow rhythmic motion. Their bodies moved in sync as if they instantly remembered what it was like to be joined as one. A spasm shook through his entire body when Adrianna's body began convulsing. He held on tight, bracing them both against the wall as they both rode an orgasmic wave of seismic proportions. When it was over, Dante gently lowered her back to her feet.

Adrianna felt hot and light-headed and before she could speak, Dante swept her up in his arms and carried her off to his bedroom.

Chapter 4

Adrianna awoke to the feel of a male hand splayed possessively across her midsection and soreness in between her thighs. She was startled at first until the memory of the night she'd spent in Dante's arms came flooding back.

Making love to him had been as good as she remembered. No, better. There was no hesitancy in his touch; he was a man confident in his ability to please her. And please her he had—she'd come twice. Dante had released a passion in her that had been buried. For the past ten years, she'd rarely dated and had buried her sexuality under a mound of regrets.

Her eyes traveled to the empty condom packets on the nightstand. There would be no pregnancies this time around; Dante had made sure to take precautions. But how would he feel if he found out the real reason she'd left him all those years ago? What if he found she'd been pregnant and had never told him? He would never forgive her for having knowingly kept his child from him after he'd grown up as an orphan.

She should have never allowed herself to get carried away last night, but it had felt so great to be kissed and touched again and not just by any man, but by Dante. Despite her marriage and a couple of failed relationships, she'd never truly gotten over Dante, her first love. At nineteen, somehow he'd gotten under her skin and she'd never been free since.

But it was best now that she keep this one beautiful memory and quickly get out of dodge, before the truth came out. Adrianna couldn't bear it if he looked at her with the same contempt she'd seen when he'd walked into her office at *Foodies*.

Slowly, she slid his hand away and crept out of bed to retrieve her clothes that had been strewn across his bedroom and the hallway. She was nearly dressed and searching for her purse, when she glanced up to find Dante standing in his boxer-briefs glaring at her with her purse in his hand.

"Looking for this?" He held up her purse.

"Thanks." Adrianna went to reach for it, but he drew back.

"Was last night one for the road? Were you planning on running away again without a word?" he asked.

"It… It's late and I've got to get to work," Adrianna murmured. "I was just getting out of your way."

"No, what you were doing was running. What you do best, Adrianna. And I don't why I should be surprised." He tossed the purse to her and headed down the hall.

"What is that supposed to mean?" Adrianna didn't know where he was going so she followed behind him. She found him in the kitchen rummaging through his cabinets.

When he produced a canister of coffee and filters, Adrianna watched as he measured out several large tablespoons and added water to the coffee machine.

"It means you're a coward," Dante finally said, turning around. His eyes flashed with outrage as they bore down on her. "When something gets too tough for you, Adrianna, you turn around and run for safety. When are you finally going to live and take a risk?"

"How can you say that? I took a risk by coming with you last night." Had she thought with her mind and not her body, she would have taken a cab home from the bar.

"And in the morning light, your first thought was to hightail it out of my bed. Why? Had you already tired of slumming it again?"

"Of course not. I've never looked down on you, Dante. I've always thought of you as my equal." From the moment they'd met in cooking class, Adrianna had been enthralled with Dante. She hadn't cared that he shared an apartment in Brooklyn with his friends and she'd grown up with a silver spoon in her mouth. She'd just wanted him and last night had been no different.

"Didn't you?" he asked indignantly. "Isn't that the reason you slinked off and married someone from a prominent family when you claimed you loved me?"

"I married him because I had to."

"Because you had to be perfect Adrianna Wright, fit nice and neatly into a box, am I right? Well, listen, I'm not going to go down this path with you. I made that mistake once and I'm not doing it again. Last night was great. Clearly the passion is still there, but let's just call it one for old time's sake and move on."

Adrianna felt as if he'd punched her. Had last night and the intimacy they'd shared meant nothing to him? "Is that really what you want?"

Dante turned his back. "Yes."

"Then fine." He was right. It was for the best. Why open old wounds? They'd merely started to take off the bandage. Had they ripped it off entirely, the bleeding would never stop. "Thanks for the memories."

And with those final words, she left. When Dante turned back around, she was gone and all he was left with was the scent of her perfume on his skin.

Adrianna crept into her father's house just before 8:00 a.m. She thought she'd make it up to her room and shower before anyone noticed, but their butler, Nigel, caught her on the staircase on the way up to her room.

"Good morning, Ms. Adrianna."

Adrianna colored. She was completely embarrassed at having been caught coming in the house after spending the night out. "Good morning, Nigel," she said slowly, turning around to face him.

"Would you care for some breakfast?"

"Uh, no." Adrianna lowered her head, shielding her eyes from his gaze. "Just coffee would be great."

"I'll bring it up right away."

Nigel stepped away to do her bidding, but Adrianna called after him. "Nigel, how was Father's night?"

"Not so great, I'm afraid. He tossed and turned all night and the nurse could not get him comfortable. He asked for you."

Adrianna felt horrible for not being at his side. She'd come back to New York to care for her father, but instead what was she doing? She was off sleeping with Dante and going after television hosting jobs she was never going to get. "I'm so sorry, Nigel. I promise I will be here tonight to make sure he's comfortable."

"If you don't mind my saying, Mr. Howard is so happy to have you back, Ms. Adrianna. You have no idea how lonely he's been since Ms. Vanessa passed away two years ago."

Adrianna had some idea, because she'd felt the same way. Her mother had been the glue that had held their family together and once she'd gone, it had been hard for Adrianna to act like her father hadn't changed the entire course of her life. In a way, she'd hated him for it and now she would have to make her peace with him before he left this earth. "Well, I'm here now."

"I'll go get the carafe of coffee," Nigel said as he left.

"Thank you, Nigel." Adrianna quickly rushed up the stairs.

Dante was pounding out several chicken cutlets for the chicken cordon bleu bites on the dinner menu that night at his namesake restaurant that night when Malik, Quentin and Sage walked into his kitchen.

"What are you guys doing here?" Dante asked as he proceeded to pound another chicken breast within an inch of its life.

"Hold up a sec, lumberjack." Quentin grabbed the mallet out of Dante's hand. "It's time we had a talk."

"Talk about what?" Dante continued to the next task of grating the Gruyère cheese that would go inside the bites since Quentin had taken his mallet away. He had to keep moving, otherwise he was going to go insane with thinking about beautiful, lying, passionate, deceitful Adrianna.

"Talk about the fact that the love of your life suddenly reappeared," Sage said, getting right to the point. "And how you feel about that." She remembered the damage Adrianna Wright had done to Dante the first time around and intended to make sure she didn't get another shot. She'd contacted Malik and Quentin so they could have a no-nonsense chat with Dante, especially since Malik had revealed that Dante might still have feelings for her.

"That's exactly what I don't want to talk about."

"C'mon, man, Sage is right," Malik added. "That woman broke your heart."

Dante rolled his eyes. "Thanks a lot."

"Well, she did." Malik was unapologetic about being honest. "And you haven't been right since."

"And now suddenly she's back out of the blue? You've gotta be confused," Quentin said.

"She's not back out of the blue," Dante replied. "Her father is dying and she's here to take care of him."

"So that's why she showed her face in Manhattan after ten years," Sage responded derisively, rolling her eyes upward. "Well, at least there's a heart somewhere in that block of ice."

"Sage, I really don't want to talk about this," Dante reiterated and started slicing prosciutto.

"Why not?" Malik asked. "Do you have something to hide?"

Dante stopped slicing, long enough to turn around to face his family. "How about the fact that we slept together last night?" He swirled around to return to his task.

"You did what?" Sage was floored and fell back against the counter.

"You heard right. The woman got under my skin."

"I thought you were upset that she could take the

hosting gig away from you. How did…" As soon as Sage said the words, she paused. She knew exactly how anger could lead to passion. She and Ian had had a few such moments in the early stages of their relationship.

"Well, I'm glad I don't have to explain the birds and the bees or that the opposite of hate is love, Sage," Quentin said with a sigh. "That talk hadn't been fun when you were a kid and I have no desire to repeat it."

Sage chuckled. She'd remembered all too well. She'd been nine when she'd gone to the fellas and asked them to explain the birds and the bees. Sure, she'd read the books and one of the headmothers of the orphanage had tried to explain, too, but how else to understand why a boy in the third grade pulled her hair one day and brought her a cupcake the next.

"As much as you protest, Dante," Quentin replied, "you're still hung up on this woman."

"I'm not hung up on Adrianna," Dante responded sharply. He began assembling layers of prosciutto and Gruyère cheese over the chicken and rolling them into a pinwheel.

"But you fell into bed with her after you'd vowed to hate her. Where does this leave your relationship now?" Malik wondered aloud.

"Nowhere," Dante stated emphatically. "All Adrianna knows how to do is run and I refuse to be stepped on for a second time. I told her as much this morning."

"I'm sure that didn't go over well," Quentin said. "No woman wants to be considered a one-night stand."

That was usually Dante's experience as well, but Adrianna had been different. "The exact opposite," he responded. "She seemed relieved that I was letting her off the hook, that I wasn't expecting anything other than the evening we shared."

Quentin frowned. "That doesn't seem right."

"No, it doesn't. Clearly, she has something to hide." As an attorney, Sage could read between the lines of what the men were failing to consider. "Something she doesn't want you to uncover. If she's been divorced for years, why did she stay away so long? She could have come back to New York before now, before her father became ill. Something just isn't right." Sage was determined to find exactly what that was. She may not have had the resources ten years ago, but she sure had them now. She wouldn't let Adrianna get away with hurting Dante again.

"What could she possibly be hiding that would have any effect on Dante at this late date?" Malik asked.

Sage shrugged. "Call me crazy, but it's only my opinion."

"Doesn't matter," Dante replied, "because last night was a temporary lapse in judgment. Adrianna and I ended nearly a decade ago and the situation hasn't changed."

"So, I came looking for you the other night at Uncle Howard's," Madison said to Adrianna when her cousin met her at a local cappuccino bar on Friday afternoon in Soho. They'd come to search the galleries for some paintings to add to Madison's loft. Madison had claimed she needed help selecting some prints, but Adrianna suspected Madison wanted to dish on gossip. "But you weren't home."

Adrianna lowered her head as images of her and Dante making love in his king-sized bed flashed in her mind.

"So where were you?" Madison asked. When Adrianna looked down and didn't answer right away, Madison shouted, "No, no, no!"

Adrianna nodded. She wasn't in the mood to be coy. If she couldn't talk to Madison about being intimate with Dante, who could she talk to? "Oh yes…"

"How?"

"You don't need me to tell you how we ended up in bed."

"Of course not. It's just a shock seeing as how the man swore he'd hate you forever. You hadn't seen how upset he'd been when he'd shown up at our apartment back then looking for you. He was absolutely furious with you."

Adrianna didn't know how to explain it, either. She hadn't seen Dante in years, but yet one look, one word, one touch from him and she was nineteen again, enthralled with the chef with the expressive brown eyes that could whip her into a frenzy with a single kiss.

"Madison. This took me by surprise as well. I never expected to fall back into old patterns with Dante, but last night something just ignited between us." She sipped on her hazelnut cappuccino.

"Something? Girl, I call that passion and apparently you guys have it in spades."

"One minute we're bickering about fighting for the same hosting gig."

"The one you told me about for Lawrence Enterprises?"

"The very one."

"Dante is up for the same position and on top of that his oldest and dearest friend is dating Ian Lawrence." Madison tore off a piece of the scone she'd ordered and plopped it in her mouth. "Sage Anderson was Dante's friend. Why I didn't put the two pieces together sooner?"

"Well, it has been quite a while," Adrianna replied. "Anyway, once I found out about it, I bombed my taping."

"I thought you were just going for an interview?"

"That's what I thought, too," Adrianna said with a humorless chuckle. "So imagine my surprise when the interviewer told me I had to cook my signature truffle macaroni and cheese in my new red Dior suit."

"You cooked mac-and-cheese in couture?"

Adrianna laughed. "I sure did. I wanted to prove that I could do anything that Dante could do. But what was even more surprising was when I ended the taping, Dante was waiting for me. We went out for cocktails and before I knew it…"

"One thing led to another," Madison finished. "So, what now? Are you guys going to pick up where you left off?"

Adrianna shook her head. "Like it would be that easy. In the cold light of day, we both realized it was a mistake, a lapse in judgment and that we should both go our separate ways."

"Girlfriend, if you could see the look on your face. You two are far from over."

"You and I both know we have to be." Adrianna sipped on her cappuccino. "If Dante ever knew the real reason I married Phillip and hightailed it out of town, he'd never forgive me."

"The miscarriage was hard on you, wasn't it?"

Adrianna sighed. "You have no idea, Madison. There I was, forced into a marriage with a man I didn't love to appease my father and to avoid being penniless only to lose the one thing I wanted most in the world, Dante's child."

"You sound like you blame yourself."

"Honestly? Sometimes, I do," Adrianna replied. "I

know the doctor said these things happen with first-time mothers, but with the stress I was under? Who knows what harm I did? Maybe God was punishing me."

"You're being too hard on yourself, Adrianna. You did the best you could for your baby at the time. And I might not be the most religious person, but I doubt God punishes people that way."

Adrianna hung her head low. "Does it really matter? Can you imagine what Dante would think of me if he knew? I had every intention of keeping his child from him, a man who grew up with no parents. He would be crushed."

"So you're just going to act like you don't have any feelings for the man? Push them down?"

"Yes, I have to."

"Well, my dear, that might have been easier if you hadn't slept with the man." Madison laughed derisively.

Adrianna sucked in a deep breath. "Tell me something I don't know."

"Thank you for agreeing to come over," Sage said when Dante arrived to Ian's penthouse for dinner on Saturday night. She was doing her best to make things right for Dante. He deserved this hosting gig. It was his time to shine and she was going to do everything in her power to make it happen—even if that meant twisting her man's arm.

"Sage, I told you to not get involved in this," Dante said when she closed the door.

"You do know who you're talking to?" Sage asked. "When have you known me to ever drop something I feel strongly about?"

Dante thought about it for a moment and chuckled. "Never." Sometimes Sage could be like a dog with a bone; she never gave up, especially when it came to their family.

"All right, then." Sage looped her arm through his as they walked through the foyer. "Come in and let's convince Ian he's making the biggest mistake of his life if he hires that two-timer."

They found Ian in the living room at the bar fixing himself a drink. "Can I get you something, Dante?" Ian asked as he poured himself a glass of Scotch.

"Rum and Coke please," Dante replied, plopping down on the Italian leather sofa.

"I'll have a vodka and tonic," Sage offered without being asked and sat next to Dante.

"Oh, that's your serious drink. I know I'm in trouble now." Ian laughed from behind the bar as he prepared the beverages.

"Not as long as you do what I want." Sage smiled back at her boyfriend.

"As much as I'd love to appease you, my pet—" Ian walked toward her with a decanter in hand "—this is business."

"Thank you." Sage accepted the proffered cocktail. "And you've never mixed business with pleasure before?" As she recalled, that's exactly how their relationship had begun.

"Do you guys need me to leave?" Dante asked, looking back and forth between the two of them. "Because I could swear this was about me."

"And you're correct, Dante," Ian replied, taking a seat opposite him in the arm chair. "You did a fabulous job during your taping. You have presence and a real charisma on-screen."

"See, I told you." Sage hit Dante's knee.

"But we saw something in Adrianna Wright, too," Ian added. "She may not be as polished as you, but then again you've been in the kitchen for years."

Dante sighed. "I see." Though he really didn't. Despite the feelings he may or may not have for Adrianna, he was a realist. Adrianna had admittedly tanked, but he'd knocked it out of the ballpark. So why would Ian choose to go with a cooking novice?

"So let me understand this correctly. You're giving the hosting job to Adrianna?" Sage was livid.

"No, I'm not," Ian replied. "I'm giving the job to Dante *and* Adrianna."

Dante was puzzled and his mouth became tight and grim. "I don't understand, Ian."

"I'd like you both to host the show."

"Excuse me?" Dante couldn't believe his ears. "I don't think so." He didn't want to share the spotlight and least of all with Adrianna.

"My staff and I think it's a brilliant idea. It would be almost like the chef teaching the newbie cooking, though not necessarily as Adrianna did go to culinary school."

"Absolutely not!" Sage stood up. "No way. How could you even think of such an insane idea? After everything I told you."

Dante's head popped up and he glared up at Sage. "Exactly what did you tell him, Sage?" He rose from the sofa. He didn't need his little sister to fight his battles. He was a grown man, for God's sake. "Sometimes you just don't know when to quit." Dante headed for the doorway.

"Dante, wait!" Sage ran after him. She caught him in the foyer. "Listen, I'm sorry, okay? I didn't go into detail with Ian about your past with Adrianna. I just told him that this woman hurt you and to make his decision carefully."

Dante's brow rose. "Are you sure about that?"

Sage crossed her heart. "I promise."

"Fine, but that doesn't change anything. He wants me to host a show with a woman who, although I'm attracted to, I'm not sure I like very much and sure as hell don't trust with my future."

"What can I do?" Sage asked.

Dante was about to answer, but Ian had joined them in the hallway. "Nothing," Ian answered. "But what Dante can do is meet me and Todd for lunch to discuss it further. What do you say?"

"I won't change my mind, Ian." Dante was firm in his decision to keep a wide berth from Adrianna for his own sanity.

"I promise if you attend I will make it worth your while."

"And will Adrianna be attending this meeting?"

Ian nodded. "Naturally."

Dante mulled it over in his head. Despite his distaste for working with Adrianna, who knew when the next opportunity to host his own television show would come up? "Fine. I'll hear you out."

"Good." Ian offered his hand. Reluctantly, Dante shook it. "My assistant Jeffrey will call you and set it up."

"See ya, kid." Dante kissed the top of Sage's forehead and gave her a quick hug before leaving.

Once he'd made it inside the town car outside, Dante wanted to scream. Adrianna had previously departed from his life without a word and now somehow she was creeping back into every aspect of it, from personal to professional. With great difficulty, he'd exorcised her once from his heart, but he wasn't so certain he could do it again. Not if he had to deal with her every day.

Chapter 5

Adrianna was excited when she got the call on Monday from Lawrence Enterprises; they wanted to see her again the following day. She'd thought she'd completely blown her taping last week and that she was out of the running for the hosting gig, but if the call was any indication she wasn't out yet.

Did this mean that Dante was out of the running?

True to his word, Adrianna hadn't heard from Dante since they'd slept together and it had been nearly a week. Although she'd admitted that it wasn't a wise idea at the time, it was hard not to think about him. She still had feelings for Dante, feelings that had bubbled up to the surface when she'd seen him again after nearly a decade, feelings that hadn't gone away since the night she'd spent in his arms. Often during the week as she'd helped feed her father or assisted him with his physical therapy so his bones didn't atrophy, her mind would wander to Dante.

What was he doing? How was he feeling? Was he thinking about her as much as she was about him? She guessed she would never know the answer to that question because Dante said he never wanted to have anything to do with her. Had she truly sunk so low in his eyes that he couldn't bear to look at her?

She walked into Le Cirque on Fifty-Eighth Street dressed sensibly in a designer pantsuit with Michael Kors pumps and feeling confident that she was once again in control—until she saw Dante sitting with Ian Lawrence and Todd Allen.

Dante watched as Adrianna approached the table with a look of utter shock. Clearly, she hadn't been informed to expect him at the meeting, but at least he'd known she was coming. Dante *almost* felt sorry for her, but then he remembered why he'd agreed to attend this lunch. Ian and Todd wanted to discuss the idea of he and Adrianna cohosting a show. A gig he wasn't all that crazy about, especially if it put him in close proximity to Adrianna day in and day out.

The men rose when Adrianna made it to the table, but it was Dante that held out her chair for her.

"Thank you." Adrianna gave him a questioning look over her shoulder. "Gentlemen." She nodded to all once she was seated.

The waiter immediately came over and filled Adrianna's water glass. "Would you care for anything to drink, miss?"

"Iced tea would be great, thanks," Adrianna replied. She turned to the men at the table. "Now would someone care to tell me why we're all here?"

"Of course," Todd replied. "We called you here today,

Adrianna, because Ian and I have a great idea for the show."

"Really?" Adrianna perked up. "I'm all ears."

"We'd like you and Dante to host the show together."

"Have you lost your mind?" Adrianna blurted out.

Ian chuckled. "Actually no, I haven't." Knowing their history together, he wasn't fazed by Adrianna's response. He'd expected as much since he was catching her off guard with his offer. "We've given this some thought and after reviewing both your tape segments, we think you'd both be an excellent addition to the WTTG family."

"I appreciate the sentiment, Ian, but this isn't going to work." Adrianna rose from the table.

Dante stood up as well. He had a few minutes prior to discuss the show before Adrianna arrived, but having her so close was already starting to play with his emotions. "I'm actually going to have to agree with Adrianna on this one, Ian. I know you mean well, but…"

Before they could both walk away, Ian blurted out, "I am prepared to offer you both one million dollars each to tape half a season which approximates to about a dozen episodes. Should they take off, we would renegotiate your salary at that time."

"Are you serious?" Dante was shocked.

The outrageous sum caused Adrianna to sit down immediately. "Did you just say one million dollars?" Adrianna couldn't believe her ears—that was more than she made in a year at *Foodies*.

"That's right." Ian watched Adrianna do the math in her head. "That equates to almost one hundred thousand per episode."

"Ian, that's insane," Todd spoke up. "We've never even offered our news anchors that kind of deal."

"Well, that's how much I believe in the two of them." Ian pointed to Dante and Adrianna. "I believe you both have what it takes to really put WTTG on the map which is why you must both accept the offer."

"And if we don't?" Dante asked, folding his arms across his chest. He didn't like to be bullied. Least of all by someone he considered a friend.

"Then the deal is off the table," Ian answered. "You have forty-eight hours to decide."

"Are you seriously giving us a deadline?" Dante was amazed by Ian's audacity.

"Yes," Ian replied, standing up and rebuttoning his suit jacket. "I take this matter very seriously and if you're not ready for the challenge, then I will go to the next people on my list. Either way, it's up to you. Have lunch on me and consider the option. Todd—" he looked to his head of production "—are you coming?" He didn't wait for a response and headed for the exit.

From the look of bewilderment on Todd's face, he clearly thought they would be having lunch at the establishment, but that wasn't the case. "Ian must really believe in you to offer such a deal," Todd offered on his way out. "If I were you I would consider it very carefully before turning it down."

The two left, leaving Adrianna and Dante alone, much to Dante's chagrin.

"So now what do we do?" Adrianna asked, returning to her seat and reaching for her glass of iced tea. She took a generous sip while she recovered from the shock she'd just received.

"Nothing has changed, Adrianna," Dante responded quietly. "I meant what I said the other morning." She'd put him through enough and he had no desire to walk down that path again. What if she ran away again once they'd started because things got too difficult? No, he was making the right decision and would avoid making a deal with the devil.

"You hate me so much that you're willing to walk away from your dream?" Adrianna glared at Dante across the table as she tried to find the man she'd once loved, but his eyes were cloudy and she couldn't read him. "And to make me lose mine?" Adrianna really wanted this and Dante was standing in her way. "Wow! You must really want to get back at me and now's your chance, huh? I hurt you, so now you hurt me?"

"Don't act so self-righteous, Adrianna," Dante returned. "You act as if I don't have the right to be angry with you, as if you don't deserve my contempt."

"You're right. Maybe I do deserve it, but never in a million years would I think that the Dante I once knew would behave this way." Adrianna stood up abruptly, causing her chair to crash to the floor. She didn't care that several people were looking at her because she was livid with Dante. She grabbed her purse and prepared to leave. "I hope you choke on your revenge," she tossed over her shoulder before storming out of the restaurant.

"Great!" Dante slammed his fists against the table.

"So, Ian wants you to host a gig with Adrianna?" Malik asked once he'd arrived to Dante's after a frantic call was placed to him that afternoon. The restaurant was closed as the staff prepared for dinner.

"I could strangle that bastard," Dante replied, pacing the floor. "When Ian initially suggested that I host this show, he acted as if it was set in stone, as if I had it in the bag. Next thing I know, I'm being 'interviewed' by the head of production and there are other candidates? What the heck is that?"

"I agree, man," Malik replied. "He should have told you that you weren't the only act in town, but at least this opportunity would get your foot in the door."

"With Adrianna?" Dante shouted. "Can you imagine having to see one of your exes every day at work? Not to mention one that you just had sex with? It would be awkward as hell."

Malik sighed. "No, I can't imagine that would be any fun."

"Oh, and did I mention that Ian offered us both one million dollars for the gig?"

"A million dollars?" Malik was stunned by the outrageous sum.

"Yes, but we must both agree to the deal or no dough."

"That's a heck of a lot of money, Dante. Would you really turn down this opportunity and that kind of money because of Adrianna?"

"Honestly, I don't know what I'm going to do," Dante responded. "I feel like I'm between a rock and a hard place. Anywhere I turn it's difficult. Do I let go of my dream and wait for the next gig because of who is attached to the show? Or do I pursue it, even though it means dealing with the woman that tore my heart in two?"

"I wish I had the answer for you, Dante," Malik replied, "but there is no easy solution here. Only you can decide what you're willing to live with."

"Where have you been going these days?" Adrianna's father asked that evening as they watched an old black-and-white movie in his bedroom. He was resting in his four poster bed while she sat in a nearby chair. "Nigel tells me you're not always home."

"I had to take care of some things," Adrianna answered, not offering any further information. It was no business of his where and with whom she was.

"Getting back to your old ways, I see," he mumbled underneath his breath.

Adrianna turned to face him. "What is that supposed to mean, Daddy?" She had hoped that they could have a peaceful evening together, but apparently that was not going to be the case.

"I remember you being this secretive when you were nineteen and do you recall the result of your actions back then?"

"Well, I'm not nineteen anymore, Father," Adrianna returned perhaps a little too harshly.

"No, you're not, which is why you must be careful not to fall back into old patterns."

"If you mean hooking up with Dante Moore you needn't worry, Father, because he wants nothing more to do with me thanks to you."

"So you have seen him since you've been back?" he inquired.

"Yes, I have."

"And you blame me for your estrangement?"

"Of course I do. You forever changed the course of my life."

"For the better I think. I doubt Moore would have been ready to be a father and husband when he was barely out of culinary school. How would he have supported you both? Plus, you know how it was back then. A scandal would have ruined my chance to become reelected as governor. It seems scandals barely seem to faze politicians or celebrities these days, but it wasn't that way a decade ago."

"See, that's the problem, Dad. You refuse to admit that

you were or could ever be *wrong*. Had you not threatened to disown me, I would be with the man I love and possibly with the child I lost."

Her father somehow found the strength to sit up and looked at Adrianna. "Do you honestly blame me for your miscarriage?"

"Partially, yes, because of the stress you caused during the early stages of my pregnancy. But most of all I blame myself."

"Adrianna, come, sit here." Her father patted the space next to him on the bed.

Reluctantly, Adrianna walked toward him and sat down.

"These things happen sometimes, baby girl. Sometimes they have no rhyme or reason and cannot be explained, but you did your best and were going to provide the child with a safe and stable home. You have to stop beating yourself up."

"Well, that's pretty hard to do when the man you once loved—" *and still do,* she thought "—despises you and with good right. I married Phillip, a man I didn't love and who only married me to further his own political aspirations. Phillip despised the fact that I had my own ambitions and craved independence. It was a marriage made in hell."

Her father hung his head low. "All I have ever wanted is the best for you, Adrianna. And perhaps I didn't go about it the right way back then and I'm sorry for that."

Tears sprang to Adrianna's eyes. She couldn't believe her ears. Her father was admitting that he was wrong. It was a hugely important step. Who knew how much time he had left on this earth? Adrianna couldn't live with herself if she didn't try to do everything in her power to mend their relationship before he passed away.

"Thank you, Father," she said through eyelashes laced with tears. "It means a lot." They were finally making progress.

Dante sat up half the night thinking about what Malik had said. There was no easy solution. Was he being too proud and stubborn if he didn't take the offer? Would he be shooting himself in the foot if he turned it down? Would he potentially regret his decision?

He'd worked his entire life to get to this point. He'd sacrificed his personal life in favor of building his career, never really getting too close to any women because he was building his reputation, but now he owned two successful restaurants. Would accepting Ian's deal make him ambitious and selfish? Of course, that's how successful, arrogant men like Ian got to where they were. Perhaps it was time he went after what belonged to him and let the chips fall where they may.

Eventually, Dante's mind quieted and he drifted off to sleep.

Adrianna was up at dawn watching the sun come up over the horizon. She'd slept miserably the previous evening and it had nothing to do with her father. She could kick herself for overreacting to Dante's less than enthusiastic response to working with her. Could she blame him for his animosity toward her? Would she want to work with him if the shoe had been on the other foot and he'd married another woman without a word to her? She doubted it. It just hurt to have him behave so coldly toward her after all they'd once meant to each other and after they had just shared a bed.

Ian's offer was a golden opportunity that neither one of them could afford to walk away from. Perhaps she'd blown up because she needed the job more than him. With two successful restaurants, Dante was well on his way to stardom and it was just a matter of time before someone recognized his talents and put him on television. Whereas, this was a way for her to get a foot back into the kitchen and show that she was more than a reviewer, that she was a chef.

Somehow she had to convince Dante to take a chance on her. Except this time it would have little to do with the sexual attraction that they shared and more to do with two chefs working together to achieve a common goal. Adrianna just hoped that she could get through to Dante.

Later that afternoon after she psyched herself out a half a dozen times about whether Dante would slam the door in her face, Adrianna arrived at Renaissance. Usually most restaurants were hopping as they prepared for the dinner, but it was nearly three and the front of the restaurant was surprisingly quiet given they would be opening in a couple of hours.

She found a busboy coming out of the kitchen with a cart of cutlery and glassware to set the tables and asked, "Where is Dante?" He nodded toward the back which Adrianna assumed to be the kitchen. Taking a deep breath, Adrianna slowly walked toward the swinging doors and entered chaos.

Dante clearly hadn't seen her come in because he was busy yelling across the room at his sous-chef. This probably wasn't the best time to bother him, but time was running out. They had less than twenty-four hours to say yay or nay to Ian's offer. As if he sensed her presence, Dante looked up from the quail he was halving and saw her.

"Now is not a good time, Adrianna," Dante said, wiping sweat from his brow with his sleeve.

"I can see that," Adrianna replied. He should have had another sous-chef on the line helping him prepare for service. Adrianna slipped off her belted wrap jacket and tossed it across a nearby chair. "What can I do?" she asked, walking toward the counter.

Dante quirked his brow questioningly. "What do you mean?"

"Well—" Adrianna glanced around the kitchen "—it looks like you're a bit short-staffed and could use a hand."

"Are you offering?"

"Duh, I am a chef you know."

His mouth curved into an unconscious smile. "Yes, you are." He remembered being in pastry class with Adrianna. "And yes, I could use a hand. Several of my staff called off due to a case of stomach flu and I'm short-staffed for dinner tonight."

"Tell me where you need me and I'm here."

Dante knew why Adrianna was there. She wanted to speak with him about Ian's offer, but at that exact moment he didn't care. He was down two line cooks and would have to cover both jobs. He could use an extra set of hands on deck. "All right, you're on. Come over here." He led her to the sink. "Can you wash and dress the rest of these quails while I prepare the sauce that will accompany them? Then I need you to dice up all that butternut squash on the counter for my soup and get started on the pastry dough for tonight's dessert."

"Aye, aye, Captain." Adrianna saluted him before slipping on a chef's coat and apron and heading over to the sink. Quickly, she took her loose curls and twisted them in a bun on her head and donned a hair net. It was time to get down to business. Adrianna didn't see Dante glance over his shoulder at her with a wistful look.

* * *

Dante was surprised at just how well he and Adrianna worked together in the kitchen. She did everything he'd asked without question except once when she'd suggested adding an extra spice to better a new dish he was debuting as a Chef's Entrée selection. It was exactly what the dish needed to make it special.

A couple of times his eyes wandered over to where she stood at the opposite side of the kitchen rinsing off vegetables. She looked cool and sophisticated with her hair twisted in a loose updo under the hair net, wearing capris and a cashmere one-shouldered top beneath her coat and apron. Dante remembered nuzzling the nape of her neck when they'd fallen into bed last week. How time flew.

Once things had settled down and they were on the line, garnishing plates for the service, Dante bumped Adrianna with his hip. "Thanks for all your help. I don't know how I would have gotten through the night without you."

Adrianna's face broke into an open, friendly smile. "You're welcome." She hadn't seen that kind look in his eye in a long time and it filled her with happiness. Of course, she did her best to hide it. Although they were getting along now, she still had a long way to go to convince Dante to work with her on a daily basis. But tonight gave her hope that it was possible for them to work as a team.

After service ended, they finally took a break to share a glass of wine and a plate of coq au vin.

"To getting through the night," Adrianna said, holding up her wineglass.

"Cheers." Dante touched his glass to hers. "Thank you again for all your help."

Adrianna smiled. "You're welcome. I was glad I could pitch in."

"Dig in." Dante nodded to the plate of food on the counter. "I know you must be starved." The orders had been nonstop for the past four hours and they hadn't had a moment to breathe, much less grab a bite to eat.

"This is delicious," Adrianna responded after putting a forkful of the delicious chicken in her mouth. "The gravy is absolutely divine."

"Thank you. I prepared it earlier this afternoon."

"You're truly gifted, Dante." Adrianna took another sip of her red wine. "Which is why you shouldn't let the opportunity of having a television show slip through your fingers."

Dante was wondering how long it would to take for her to bring up Ian's ultimatum.

"Trust me, I know I'm not the ideal person you'd like to share this experience with." Adrianna touched her hand to her chest. "But this means a lot to me as well. And I think I was too hasty to say no the other day. Neither one of us can afford to turn our backs on this. Who knows when there might be another chance? So I'm asking you to please reconsider. If anything, tonight showed our professionalism and that we are capable of working together. So what do you say?"

Dante stood quietly as Adrianna gave her speech. He watched her lips move, but was more fascinated with the woman with whose fate his seemed intertwined. Could he, should he, take another chance on Adrianna Wright—or would she inevitably break his heart once again?

Chapter 6

Adrianna stood by with bated breath, wondering if Dante was going to shatter her dreams or take a chance on her.

"Okay," Dante conceded, taking off his chef's jacket. He was tired of fighting her. It took too much energy trying to hate Adrianna, especially when it was the exact opposite of how he felt.

Adrianna stared back at him, dumbfounded. "Okay?" Did she hear him correctly?

"I will accept Ian's offer if you do," Dante replied.

A tentative smile spread across Adrianna's face. "So you're ready to let go of the past and start fresh?"

Dante nodded.

"Ohmigod, you have no idea how happy you've made me." Adrianna rushed toward Dante and wrapped her arms around his broad shoulders.

Dante wasn't sure at first of how to react. Should he push her away? Or should he grab her and hold on for dear life? The latter won out and when they finally pulled away, a sensuous spark passed between them and called to everything male in him, causing Dante to sweep her in his arms once more. His mouth covered Adrianna's hungrily and his tongue traced the soft fullness of her lips, Adrianna's lips parted to welcome him in. His tongue mated with hers in a delicious dance that Adrianna welcomed.

Adrianna's whole being flooded with desire and the dormant sexuality of her body awakened once again. She felt her breasts crush against the hardness of his chest and her body craved his. She ran her hands down the length of his back, pulling him closer to her. There was no disguising the fact that he roused a passion in her like no other man.

When they eventually pulled away, Dante's breath was ragged and it took a moment for him to collect himself. He glanced at Adrianna and could see she had been as affected as he.

"You realize that you and I can't be *just friends*," he finally spoke after a prolonged silence.

"We could try," Adrianna offered.

"There's too much history," Dante responded. "And furthermore, I don't think I want to try."

Adrianna frowned. "So you want a purely professional relationship?" If that was what it was going to take for Dante to agree to the arrangement then Adrianna would honor his request. She wouldn't like it, but she would honor it. She stood to lose too much if she didn't agree.

Dante shook his head. "No, I don't want to be friends and don't want to be just business partners."

"Then what do you want?" He was confusing her.

"Isn't it clear enough? I want you," Dante stated. He stared back at Adrianna, his eyes raking her boldly.

"You do?"

"Yes, I do, and I know you want me," Dante replied. The moans that had escaped her mouth when he'd kissed her had been indication enough. "So, if this television show is going to work, we're going to have to be honest about what we're both feeling."

Honest. The word instantly sent fear coursing through Adrianna's veins and sent her brain into tumult. It was the one thing she couldn't be with Dante, not completely anyway. How could she tell him the real reason she'd married Phillip? If she did, he would never forgive her for trying to keep his child away from him.

Dante scrutinized Adrianna's face, but couldn't read her, so he continued. "I'm not saying we can just pick back up where we left off. But perhaps we can start anew. You know, take things slow. We can try dating and see where that takes us." Dante didn't know what to make of Adrianna's silence. Was she happy at the prospect of a relationship between them? Or would she rather they kept things professional? Had he been that far off the mark in sensing that she wanted more, too?

Adrianna's mind was swimming through a haze of feelings and desire. She knew Dante was wondering why she hadn't spoken up. She wanted to shout from the rooftops that she wanted to renew their relationship again. She'd dreamed of this moment for a decade and now that it was here, Adrianna was afraid to reach for what she wanted. What if it backfired?

"Adrianna, have you heard a word I've said?" Dante asked when she appeared dazed. "Blink if you heard me."

Adrianna blinked several times. "I heard you." Adrianna found her voice finally.

"Then what?" Dante stared back at her, baffled. He was confused by the wall Adrianna was erecting around her.

"I'm afraid."

"Of what? The future?" Dante inquired. "Because to me it looks pretty bright. We have a wonderful opportunity ahead of us that's going to give us a ton of name recognition and put us on the map. And after all these years, there's a chance for us to find out what would have been. Baby, don't you want that?"

A hot tear rolled down Adrianna's cheek. She remembered how much she'd always loved Dante calling her baby. "I do want it, Dante."

Dante walked toward her and grabbed both her hands. "Then let's do it. No looking back on the past. From this point on, we both have a clean slate. Are you ready?" He released one hand to brush away her tears.

"I am," Adrianna replied and wrapped her arms around his neck. "I am."

The next morning, Adrianna and Dante arrived to Lawrence Enterprises' corporate offices as a team, but not before he asked Sage, his attorney, to meet them at Dante's to discuss their terms.

Sage's mouth tightened when she saw a familiar face sitting at a table.

"What is Adrianna doing here?" Sage whispered, grabbing Dante by the arm and rushing him off to the coat closet. "I thought this was a business meeting?"

"It is," Dante responded, shrugging her hand away. "Didn't your boyfriend tell you about the take-it-or-leave-it deal he offered me?"

"No. I've been tied up in depositions the past couple

of days, so I've just crashed at my place. Why?" Sage glanced at Dante questioningly.

"He offered us one million dollars to share the television show. And either we both accepted within forty-eight hours of the offer or the deal was off the table."

Sage's eyes grew wide and she took a step back. "You're kidding?" She didn't care for Ian's strong-arm tactics, but it was just like him to pull a stunt like this. She remembered that he'd stopped at nothing to seduce her.

"Afraid not."

"So you had no choice but to pair up with that she-devil?" Sage stomped her foot in anger. "I could kill Ian for putting you in this position."

"Hold it a second there, Sage." Dante knew that look in her eye and it meant Sage was going to be on the warpath. "Adrianna and I have made our peace with the situation and have agreed to work together, so there's no reason for you to put your relationship on the line for me."

"But…"

"No buts." Dante pointed his finger at Sage, reminding her of the times he used to reprimand her as a child. "I don't need you to fight this battle."

Sage's mouth turned into a thin line. "Fine, but it doesn't mean I have to like it or her. She hurt you terribly."

Dante laughed aloud. "As I recall, I wasn't too happy with Ian, either, when you landed in the hospital with a severe asthma attack, but you know what? When you got back together, I sucked it up. You're going to have to do the same."

"You mean you are a couple now?" Sage asked. "Since when? Just the other day you didn't even want to speak her name."

"We're not a couple," Dante replied, "but that could change. Now let's go. We're being incredibly rude talking in the coat closet."

When Dante approached her, Adrianna's heart skipped a beat and butterflies jumped around in her belly. Dante had that kind of effect on her. Despite the past, she knew she'd made the right decision in going after the television show and Dante. She'd followed her heart.

Of course, it wasn't going to be easy convincing Dante's family that she was a changed woman if the evil eye Sage was giving her as she stalked toward the table was any indication. But try she would, because without their support, their relationship was doomed.

"Sage." Adrianna stood up and came toward her to give her a hug, but instead Sage extended a hand. Adrianna accepted it with a smile. "It's so good to see you."

"I'm not so sure I can say the same," Sage returned.

"Sage, I'm warning you," Dante muttered underneath his breath.

"Well, let's get down to business." Sage opened up her briefcase and pulled out her legal folder. "Before we go to LE let's discuss talking points."

An hour later, Dante, Adrianna and Sage were in LE's conference room with Todd and a member of Sage's firm discussing the contract.

"Sage, you're representing Mr. Moore and Ms. Wright?" her colleague asked. "With Greenberg, Hanson, Waggoner, Anderson and Associates representing LE as corporate counsel don't you think it's a conflict of interest?"

"I don't have a problem with it." Ian smiled at Sage from the doorway. He was not surprised Sage was representing Dante; he was family after all.

"Well, then neither do I," Sage's colleague responded.

"Are you both here to accept the terms I've set forth?" Ian inquired, glancing at Dante and Adrianna.

"Yes, we are," Dante and Adrianna replied in unison.

"With a few stipulations," Sage added, giving Ian a wink.

A half hour later, Dante was excited that they'd nailed the terms and that he and Adrianna would be the hosts for *Easy Entertaining* in the next two months.

"A lot of work lies ahead for the two of you," Todd said on their way out. "I'll be in touch."

"And we can't wait to get started," Adrianna replied, smiling from ear to ear.

While Dante chatted with Ian, Sage took the opportunity to pull Adrianna aside. "Just so you know, I am watching you." Sage motioned to her eyes with her index and middle fingers.

"Excuse me?" Adrianna had no idea what she meant.

"Dante has put his trust and faith in you for a second time. You had better make darn sure you don't hurt him again," Sage warned, "because if you do, you'll have to deal with me."

"I appreciate the warning, Sage," Adrianna responded. "But I have no intention of hurting him."

"Well, you make sure that's the case," Sage replied as Dante walked over.

"Everything okay here?" he asked, looking at each woman.

"Everything is fine," Adrianna stated emphatically. She would make sure of it.

"You seem nervous," Madison commented as she and Adrianna shopped at a small boutique in the Garment

District on Friday afternoon for a dress for her and Dante's first official date in ten years.

"I am," Adrianna admitted.

"Why?" Madison handed her another dress to try on as the one she was wearing was dreadful. "You've already shared a bed with Dante. I would think *that* would have made you more self-conscious."

Adrianna shook her head. "It didn't." She lifted her hair so Madison could zip the spaghetti-strapped dress. She surveyed herself in the mirror before saying, "Making love with Dante was the most natural thing in the world, but tonight is completely different."

"How so?"

Adrianna turned around to face her. "Because…we'll be really talking about who we are now. There won't be any more hashing the past back and forth. Who was wrong. Who did what to whom. We'll be really getting to know each other and I'm scared about being so open with Dante."

"Afraid you'll let something slip?"

Anxiety spurted through her and she clenched her hands until her nails dug into her palms. The past was always hanging over her head. "Maybe. And what if after dating me, he doesn't like the woman I've become now? What if after all these years, all the longing, all the unrequited dreams, we don't work out after all?"

"That's ridiculous. You're absolutely fabulous. Now take that dress off and try on this one."

"I hope Dante thinks so." Adrianna shimmied out of the skintight dress and accepted the strapless teal jersey dress Madison offered. It was a bold color and usually not her style. She usually wore black. Why was that? Since when had she stopped being the headstrong girl who'd told her parents she was going to culinary school instead of finishing school? *When she'd followed her father's directive,* that's when. She'd stopped being her and had become the person *he* wanted her to be, the socially acceptable daughter in a high-collar black dress and pearls.

"Personally, I think you're putting way too much pressure on yourself," Madison replied. "Just take it one day at a time and see what comes. Starting with that dress." The crystals along the bustline accentuated Adrianna's breasts and made them appear fuller. Dante would be dazzled.

Adrianna swirled around in the mirror and smiled. "This is definitely the one."

"Are you sure this is a good idea?" Quentin asked when he stopped by with his daughter, Bella, to drop off some new photographs for Dante to swap out at Renaissance. Quentin found him getting ready for a date with Adrianna. "Given the woman burned you the last time around?"

"Wow! I expected that kind of reaction from Sage," Dante returned, adjusting the tie that accompanied his dark blue Versace suit in the mirror. "But not from you." He was already a little apprehensive about dating Adrianna. There was a lot about her he didn't know. The last time they'd been together, there hadn't been much talking. Sure, there'd been posturing about who was going to land the talk show position, but he'd been more interested in ripping the clothes off her body. Now that he wasn't thinking with the lower part of his anatomy, he wanted to know exactly what made Adrianna tick.

"Just a few days ago you were ready to strangle the woman for running out of your bed and now you're ready to tie yourself to her in and out of bed?" Quentin shrugged as he bounced Bella up in the air and watched her giggle with excitement.

"You think I'm crazy, right?" Dante asked, turning around to face Quentin. Admittedly, he'd had second thoughts after their big talk, but the more he'd thought about it, the more he knew he had to try and see where things could go with Adrianna. Because if he didn't, he would always wonder what would have been and he'd already wasted time with other women.

Quentin smiled. "No, I don't. Men have done crazier things for love. Remember when Avery asked me not to use those negative pictures of her biological father, Richard King, in the magazine article Malik needed on the community center?"

"I remember." Dante took Bella's tiny hand in his and kissed it. Malik had wanted a scathing exposé written on entrepreneur Richard King and his intention to tear down the community center they'd all grown up in. The center had been a refuge from them when they needed to get away from the orphanage. "And Malik wasn't too happy with you for it."

"So I know just how far a man will go for love," Quentin responded. "I was willing to do anything for Avery. Still will."

"You're lucky. You and Avery never lost time together. Adrianna and I have so much time to make up for."

"Is that why you hopped into bed with her the first second you saw her?" Quentin laughed.

"Ah, man, that was lust. Plain and simple."

Dante felt a little uneasy on the drive to Adrianna's family home in the Hamptons to pick her up for dinner. Although he'd never visited, he could only imagine the estate her father owned. Howard Wright had been governor of New York State for nearly a decade before he'd retired six years ago. Mr. Wright hadn't hidden the fact that he didn't care for Dante years ago and thought he wasn't worthy of his daughter.

Back then, the shame had eaten at him. Because he grew up in an orphanage without parents, he'd felt less than, and Howard's words had only reinforced those feelings. But as time went on, Dante began to realize his own self-worth. It wasn't his fault his mother had abandoned him in a hospital as a toddler and never looked back. These days toddlers were the pick of the litter and were easily adopted because they wouldn't remember their former lives. Dante hadn't been so lucky. He'd lived in one foster home after another. Once, when he was about six, a foster family seemed like they were going to adopt him, but when the wife got pregnant all bets were off.

As he drove to the house, Dante was confident and proud of the man staring back at him in the rearview mirror. He'd come a long way from his humble beginnings. He wasn't an insecure twenty-five-year-old just finding himself. He was a grown man with two successful restaurants and a television show on the way. He was absolutely good enough for Adrianna Wright.

When he arrived at the door, a butler greeted him. Dante wasn't surprised; that was how the rich and famous lived.

"Mr. Moore, come right in," Nigel said, opening the door and motioning Dante into the foyer. "Ms. Adrianna will be down in a moment."

"Thank you."

"Would you care for an aperitif?" Nigel inquired.

Dante smiled politely. "No, but thanks."

"Very well. I will advise Ms. Adrianna you are waiting."

As he stood in the marble tiled foyer with the vaulted ceiling and rich oak woodwork, Dante could see why Mr. Wright had thought that his daughter, born to money and prestige would never settle with a poor cook. It started to make him think of the past. Thank God Adrianna floated down the stairs at that exact moment wearing a strapless dress that showed off her bosom and helped him forget all thoughts of the past.

"Wow! You look stunning," he commented, grasping her hand and twirling her around. His eyes were compelling and magnetic as they drifted across her body.

Adrianna beamed. "Thank you. You look handsome as well." She wasn't sure which designer it was, but the suit he was wearing was tailored to fit his beautifully proportioned body.

"Are you ready for our first date?" Dante's eyes clung to hers.

Adrianna thought back to their first official date twelve years ago which consisted of a movie and a New York style hot dog off a street vendor. "Oh, I'm ready." She'd waited a lifetime for this moment.

"Where are we going?" Adrianna asked once she was seated in Dante's town car and they were driving back into Manhattan from the Hamptons.

"I have special surprise for you," Dante said.

They arrived a short while later to Daniels on Park Avenue and the valet assisted Adrianna out of the car. They walked inside the eighteen-foot ceiling restaurant done with sleek contemporary furnishings and Adrianna was impressed. She hadn't been to Daniels since they redesigned the interior in 2008. The new etched glass light boxes encompassing the balustrades and chandeliers lit up the main dining room while Renaissance paintings and creamy silk panels adorned the walls. Adrianna was impressed by the renovation.

"Are they closed for the evening?" Adrianna asked, glancing around the empty restaurant.

Dante smiled. "They are closed exclusively for us."

Adrianna couldn't believe Dante had gone through the trouble of shutting down an entire restaurant just for them. "Dante, this is too much."

"Nothing is too much for you."

"Mr. Moore, pleasure to have you here with us again," the maitre d' said as they walked to the host counter.

Dante shook his hand. "Pleasure as always, Jacques. Is our table ready?"

"Yes, it is."

"Lead the way." Dante grasped Adrianna's hand and a tingle went up her arm at the tiny action. The evening meant so much to her. To finally be able to spend time with Dante after all these years was a blessing and Adrianna intended to enjoy every minute of it.

Instead of the maitre d' sitting them at one of the empty tables, he escorted them past the main dining room to the kitchen.

"Will I be cooking my own meal?" Adrianna asked, laughing as memories of her cooking her truffle macaroni and cheese in Dior came to mind. "Because if so, I should have a worn a different outfit."

Dante's eyes roved her lithe body up and down. "I like the one you're wearing just fine," he replied. "And no, you won't be cooking your own meal, but you will be watching Chef Boulud finish cooking the meal right in front of you."

"Seriously?" Adrianna's eyes grew wide with excitement. "I have always wanted to meet him. His food is a work of art."

"Then you're in for a real treat." Dante smiled at her.

The maitre d' led them to exclusive table that had been set up for them in the kitchen. The table was beautifully arranged with tiger lilies—her favorite flower—along with the finest crystal she'd ever seen.

Dante helped Adrianna into her seat as she glanced around for Chef Boulud. "This is truly special, Dante. Thank you."

"You're welcome."

"Glass of champagne?" The maitre d' asked, holding a bottle of expensive French champagne in front of them.

"Yes, please," Dante answered.

"How did you meet Chef Boulud?"

"When I was nominated for a James Beard Award years back, he was kind of a mentor to me."

Adrianna wasn't surprised at just how accomplished Dante was; she could only hope she would make him shine on the television show.

"That James Beard nomination must have been a huge honor for you."

"I know some people only give lip service to say it was an honor to be nominated, but for me, it was. An orphan who grew up with nothing? It was incredibly gratifying to be recognized for my work but I'm not the only accomplished one. You've done so much as well. You're *Foodies'* top reviewer and feared by chefs all around the country."

Adrianna laughed. "A little fear is always good because it keeps the chefs on their toes. My job isn't always easy, you know. Not every dish is perfection. Imagine when you have to try something god-awful." She wrinkled her nose.

"Well, you won't have that problem here," Chef Boulud said from behind her.

Instantly, Adrianna rose to her feet. "Chef, it is an honor." She bowed. With numerous accolades and restaurants in New York, Palm Beach, Vegas and London, the French chef with the salt-and-pepper hair was world renowned for his soulful cooking.

"No need to bow," he said in a rich French accent and smiled warmly at her. "I have prepared an excellent feast for your senses, starting off with my hazelnut-crusted sea scallops with green peppercorn sauce, followed by Maine crab salad and then on to the main event—a trio of farm veal with tenderloin, sweetbreads and cheeks with some young turnips. Perfection!" He kissed his fingertips.

"Sounds wonderful, Chef. We look forward to the meal," Dante said. "And thank you so much for agreeing to this on one of your nights off."

"Ah, I appreciate true romance," he said to the duo. "So enjoy."

Dante and Adrianna spent the evening eating the best in French cuisine while reminiscing on culinary school and catching up on the past ten years of each other's lives.

After a while, Adrianna wasn't so nervous about whether or not Dante would like the thirty-one-year-old version of her. Over the years, they'd only matured and what they once loved about each other, like their common interest in cooking, action movies, jazz and the New York Yankees, was only reinforced.

At one point, Dante leaned over and fed her some hazelnut-crusted scallop.

"Hmm." Adrianna licked her lips. She was starting to feel more relaxed when out of the blue Dante asked her how long she'd been married. At first she didn't want to answer, but Dante was waiting so she said, "About three years."

"That wasn't very long," Dante commented, taking a forkful of the second course of crab salad. "What happened?" He was curious. If the marriage hadn't lasted long why had she not come back to New York before now? What had kept her away?

"Do you really want me to talk about this?" Adrianna had hoped that this evening would focus on their future, not their past.

"It was a part of your life that I'd like to know about."

"Marriage wasn't what I thought it was going to be."

"How so?"

"Phillip only married me for political advantage and I married him because it's what my father wanted." It wasn't completely the truth, but it was close enough. "For years, I tried so hard to be the person everyone expected me to be. During my marriage, I had to be the perfect socialite wife, keeping the perfect house and hosting the best dinner parties, and I lost sight of who I was. And as I grew older, I realized I didn't have to conform to anyone else's image of me."

"Is that when you went to Le Cordon Bleu in Paris?"

Adrianna grinned as a memory of the chefs at the French school putting her through the ringer came to mind. "Yes, I guess I had to prove that I could do something on my own, be my own person, be independent, and try new things."

"Then our next destination will fit the bill for you," Dante said.

The town car coursed through the streets of Manhattan and stopped in front of a two-story building in Midtown.

"Where are we?" Adrianna asked when the driver came around to open her door.

"You'll see." Dante rushed her inside the building.

As they climbed the flight of stairs, Adrianna heard the distinct sounds of Latin music. When they reached the door, she could see that the sign read Dance Sport. He brought her to a dance studio? Why?

"C'mon." Dante grabbed her hand and opened the door.

A large group of dancers were already assembled and swaying across the dance floor.

"Why did you bring me here?" Adrianna asked. She'd learned to waltz with her father and that was because he led, but that was the extent of her dance experience.

"So we can tango," he replied smoothly, taking off his suit overcoat. "You need to learn to let loose and have some fun."

Adrianna was about to respond that she knew how to have fun, but when was the last time she'd been out dancing with anyone? Her ex-husband certainly hadn't enjoyed it. He'd been more content to read a newspaper or watch a political television show.

"Are you game?" Dante threw her a challenge.

Being with Dante was always exhilarating and Adrianna never knew what to expect. It was what made him so exciting. He was completely unlike any man she'd ever dated. "Let's go." She held out her hand.

"All right." Dante smiled and confidently walked toward her. He doubted she'd ever tangoed in her entire life, but he admired her willingness to try. He grasped her small hand and swiftly pulled her into his embrace.

Adrianna nearly lost her breath at being so close to Dante. The last time they'd been this close, they'd ended up horizontal. She stretched her right arm out into what she assumed from all the movies she'd seen was the tango position and turned to face him. When Dante slid even closer until their bodies were nearly one, Adrianna knew she was a goner.

The music started and Dante stepped forward. Adrianna followed his lead by stepping back. He repeated the dramatic movement with a sharp turn of the head and then easily slid her into a side step. Adrianna was forced to face him and came into direct contact with Dante's appreciative male gaze as he moved ahead for two forward steps. He paused momentarily before completing the same counter-clockwise flow of movements across the dance floor.

Adrianna kept up with him by mirroring his actions. At times his movements were slow and slithering like a lion on the prowl. Other times, they were sharp and staccato. It was clear Dante was in his element as this was a dance in which the man led and the woman followed.

When the music became stronger, he flung Adrianna away like a ragdoll and then drew her to him again like she was his most prized possession. The smoldering glint in his light brown eyes filled her with longing. How were they supposed to take things slow when he looked at her like that?

His burning eyes held hers throughout the dance while his fingers slid sensuously over her bare arms. He led her across the floor with ease in the slow, slow, quick, quick, slow routine before suddenly spinning her around and around. She'd barely had a chance to recover when he crushed her to him and leaned down to kiss her. It was light and soft, a mere brush of his lips, but Adrianna felt it all the same.

When they parted Dante looked into Adrianna's eyes and found the excitement had added shine to her gaze and color to her cheeks. They were so busy looking into each other's eyes that they didn't realize the music had stopped until the entire class began clapping enthusiastically.

Adrianna enjoyed the tango. The dance had shown her a different side of herself. A side in which she could be free to try something new and not care about how others saw her. For most of her life, she'd had to watch how she behaved for fear of how she would be viewed, but tonight she hadn't cared that they'd had an audience. In fact, she'd reveled in being in Dante's arms.

An older Latin woman whom Adrianna could only assume was the instructor approached them. "My dear." The woman kissed both of Dante's cheeks. "You've come a long way."

"Madeline Dubois, allow me to introduce Adrianna Wright."

"Lovely to meet you." The older woman extended a hand which Adrianna shook. "Isn't he wonderful? Dante has been taking private lessons and is my star pupil."

"Oh, really." Adrianna looked up at Dante questioningly.

"Yes." Madeline smiled. "Dante is a natural. And it looks like he's found the right partner in you. You two generated some serious heat on the dance floor just now. My students could learn a thing or two from you about passion."

Adrianna blushed.

"Madeline, thank you for allowing me to interrupt your class, but we really must be going." Dante bent down to kiss her cheek. "I promise to stay longer next time."

"I'm going to hold you to it, Dante."

Dante helped Adrianna with her wrap, slowly draping it across her shoulders. "You ready?" he whispered in her ear.

Adrianna glanced behind her. "I am, if you are."

Once in the car, Adrianna thanked Dante for the experience. "When did you learn how to tango?" she inquired. "Was it a way to get to the ladies?" She'd seen quite a few women in the dance studio.

Dante chuckled. "Is that jealousy I hear in your voice?"

"Of course not," she lied. "I was just curious."

"I learned to tango when I took waltzing with Quentin and Avery for their wedding. Poor Quentin had two left feet when it came to waltzing, but I picked it up quite easily and found I enjoyed it, so I tried another dance. First it was the tango, and then the rumba, then I got more adventurous with the cha-cha, samba and mambo."

"I'm impressed," Adrianna responded. "Not many men would venture out of their element."

"I'm not many men," Dante replied huskily.

Adrianna glanced at Dante. "No, you're not." Her eyes fixated on Dante's full sensuous lips and she knew the evening was not about to end.

"What do you say to a nightcap?" Dante asked.

"I'd love one."

Chapter 7

Back at his duplex Dante uncorked a bottle of his favorite white wine and poured Adrianna and himself a glass.

She'd already made herself comfortable on his leather sofa as she soaked in the ambiance. Dante had turned on some soft jazz on his iPod docking station and Adrianna kicked off her strappy heels and tucked her legs underneath her.

"Here you go, my dear." He returned from the kitchen to hand her the wine.

"Thank you." Adrianna accepted the glass as he joined her on the sofa. Dante didn't sit far away, either; he scooted close to Adrianna until their thighs touched, sending a tingling straight to the pit of her stomach. Dante had a raw sexuality that was lethal to her well-being.

"To a wonderful first date." She stared with longing at Dante over the rim of her glass.

"And an even better evening," Dante added, his eyes never leaving her face.

The heat between them was so intense they didn't bother to take a sip of wine. Instead Dante took the glass of out Adrianna's hands and placed it on the cocktail table. He grasped both sides of her face and kissed her, sending spirals of ecstasy straight through her.

Dante relished the feeling of having Adrianna in his arms again and groaned huskily. "Do you want me as much as I want you?" he asked, pulling her into his lap and angling himself so he could nuzzle her neck.

There was no mistaking the bulge in his pants, so Adrianna's answer was a soft sigh. She wanted nothing more than to be right where she was, lying against his wide chest.

His eyes lingered on her tantalizing pink lips, just before he bent down to suck on the fleshy bottom of her lower lip. She opened her mouth to give him full access and Dante groaned, gathering her close in his arms. Adrianna was all woman and all his and he intended to show her just how much he wanted her. The first time they'd made love here had been hurried and frantic because the passion had overtaken them, but this time it would be different. This time they could slowly savor each other's bodies and take delight in each other's responses.

Adrianna moaned as Dante made the kiss deeper and wetter than the last one. When his lips left her mouth to trail a path down her cheek to her neck and then on to the valley between her breasts, she moaned in protest. Then she felt cool air hit her back as Dante unzipped her strapless dress and pushed it down, exposing her bare breasts to his appreciative male gaze. The dress had a built-in bra so she hadn't needed one.

"Adrianna…sweet Adrianna," Dante murmured as he lowered his head and licked the dark brown nipple of one full globe. He laved the peak with his tongue until it turned hard like a plump raisin. When he was done with one globe, he turned his attention to the other and paid it equal service. "Is it good, sweetness?" he asked, his voice hoarse with desire.

Adrianna nearly screamed at the attention he was bestowing on her breasts. Red-hot flames of desire were shooting through every nerve ending and she couldn't resist letting out a purr of ecstasy. He'd pleasured her so well, she returned the favor by reaching down to stroke his shaft inside his pants.

Adrianna's soft hands caressed his length slowly at first, causing Dante to clench his teeth. Then she began quickening the strokes.

"Like this?" she asked as she pleasured him with her hand.

"Y-yes," he barely managed to get out, as she squeezed the fullness in his pants, "which is why we need to take this to the bedroom."

He lifted her, weightless in his arms, and carried her off to his bedroom. When they came down on the bed, his weight pressed her into the mattress and his mouth claimed hers again with fierceness. When she recovered her senses, he stripped her of her bikini panties and she was naked as the day she was born.

His hungry gaze roved her caramel-colored length. "I want you now," he said as he stood beside the bed and began to undress. He tossed his clothes aside with little regard because he was eager to be with Adrianna. The wanton look she was giving him as she watched him unzip his pants caused him to shove his pants and briefs down his hips quickly and kick them away.

His sex jutted out powerfully as he approached the bed, causing Adrianna to lick her lips with anticipation. She was fascinated by that male part of him and the tremendous power he possessed. "And I want you." She reached up to pull him down to join her on the bed.

His hands caressed the long expanse of her outer thighs and steadily moved forward to stroke the petal-softness of her inner thigh all while his tongue dipped in and out of her mouth. He could feel Adrianna trembling underneath him as his fingertips found their way to the hair covering her mound. He hovered at first, letting his fingers tease the plump folds, until they gently worked their way inside to worry the tiny nub at the top of her womanhood.

Adrianna moaned aloud, drawing Dante's eyes to hers. He watched her enjoyment accelerate as he played with the tiny nub. Her eyes fluttered and closed as he maddeningly caressed the sweet folds between his fingers. Her breath started coming in quick, uneven pants.

"Are you enjoying it, baby?" Dante crooned close to her ear. He could feel her become slick with her own juices. He wanted to drown in her sweet scent and taste and before Adrianna could react, his lips quickly left hers and he lowered himself on the bed to focus his attention elsewhere.

He cupped her buttocks between both hands and lifted her hips to his mouth and tongued her with feverish delight. Adrianna nearly jumped off the bed at the first flick of his tongue down there. He stroked her until she cried out with delight.

At her desperate cries to take her, Dante quickly leaned over to the nightstand to grab a condom and slip it on before he slid between her thighs and eased himself into the slick entrance of her body. He trembled with pleasure as he pressed forward and Adrianna accepted him easily. His upper body lifted off the bed as he used his hips to plunge again and again deep inside her. He reveled in her moist heat and Adrianna clung to him, calling his name and begging him for more.

Dante gave her exactly what she wanted, by thrusting harder and faster until he felt her body climax underneath him. He gave one final stroke before he, too, gave in to the sheer pleasure of his own powerful release. He collapsed on top of her before rolling over to his back and pulling her into his arms.

Adrianna didn't protest. Her curvy body was still intertwined with his and she rested her head on his shoulder.

"That was amazing," Adrianna finally spoke once she'd caught her breath.

"You're amazing," Dante murmured just as he drifted off to sleep.

The next morning, Adrianna slowly awoke to find herself in Dante's arms and this time she wasn't thinking about running away. She smiled as she turned to face him, but he was still asleep. It gave her a chance to study him unobserved.

Last night had been magnificent. Dante was the giving lover she'd remembered him to be. He knew exactly where and how to touch her to evoke a response and he made sure she was completely satisfied each time they made love. With Dante, she felt beautiful, sexy and every bit a woman.

She couldn't resist stroking his strong jawline and letting her fingertips caress the fullness of his lips. Her actions caused Dante's eyes to pop open.

"Good morning, beautiful," he said lazily.

"Good morning." She brushed her lips across his.

"Ummm," Dante moaned. "I like being woken up like that. And more importantly, I like having you in my bed." His mouth swooped down to capture hers.

When he finally lifted his head, Adrianna asked, "So what's on the agenda today?"

"You don't have to get back to your father?"

"Nigel is with him and I don't want this day to end."

Dante felt the same and was glad Adrianna did, too.

"Well then, if you're interested the New York Yankees are playing today. How about we catch a game?"

"For real?"

"Yes, one of my favorite diners works there. I always give him the best table in the house and he always tells me if I need to be hooked up, he'll take care of me."

Adrianna's eyes twinkled with amusement. "Pays to know people in high places. And it sounds great, but I have nothing to wear." She only had the dress she'd worn last night.

"Don't worry about it," he responded. "You can wear some of my old sweats and we'll pick you up something on the way."

"Sounds like a plan."

While Adrianna showered, Dante lined up plans for the day. First, they'd shop around and find Adrianna some casual clothes for the day. Then it was off to Yankee Stadium to watch the Yankees play the Boston Red Sox, followed by a romantic dinner along the Brooklyn Bridge. He'd already taken the liberty of ordering a dress from Bergdorf Goodman for their evening festivities.

Dante was waiting for Adrianna when she emerged from the steaming hot shower, holding a fluffy white towel. Adrianna wasn't embarrassed stepping out of the shower and into his arms. Dante knew every part of her now, intimately.

Dante bent down and licked a droplet of water off Adrianna's glistening skin as he dried off her wet body. "Hmmm, you smell fresh and clean."

"Yeah, well, you'd better stop that or we'll end up back in bed."

Dante's face melted into a buttery smile. "And would that be such a bad thing?" He couldn't get enough of her sweetness. It was like she had him under her spell and he was powerless to resist.

They eventually made it out of his condo on the Upper West Side to head to a department store to pick out Adrianna something to wear. The weather was unseasonably warm for May and they didn't need jackets. Dante was wearing a Yankees jersey, jeans and sneakers, while Adrianna was dwarfed in his old sweats and a pair of flip-flops. She'd had to roll up the legs to her ankles just to appear somewhat stylish as they walked down the street.

They arrived at Barneys and with not much time to spare, Adrianna found a tunic that cinched at the waist, some skinny jeans and a pair of bejeweled sandals to wear to the baseball game.

While she was putting on her clothes in the dressing room, Dante called his restaurants to let the staff know he would not be in. He put his sous-chefs in charge for the day.

"Are you kidding?" Marvin, his sous-chef at Dante's, said. "You're really not coming in?"

"No," Dante stated emphatically. "I'm not."

"I can't remember the last time you took a day off," Marvin commented.

"Well, then," Dante said, "you had better enjoy being top dog for the day."

He was hanging up when Adrianna came out of a dressing room stall. "How do I look?"

Dante's eyes roamed over her figure. He loved the way the jeans hugged her backside. "Just perfect."

"Okay, tell the sales lady I'm cutting off the tags, because this is coming with." On the way to the counter, Adrianna couldn't resist adding a hobo bag to her outfit, but when she arrived to the counter she found Dante had taken care of everything. "Dante, you didn't have to buy my clothes."

"I know. I wanted to."

"Thank you." She pulled him close for a quick kiss on the lips.

"And please put the bag on my card as well," he instructed the cashier.

When they made it outside, Dante's town car was already waiting for them and ready to take them to the game.

"Are you trying to spoil me?" Adrianna asked, sliding into the backseat.

"Yeah, how am I doing?"

"Marvelous, baby. Marvelous." Adrianna giggled. She couldn't remember the last time she'd been this happy. She felt euphoric and she had Dante to thank for it.

The drive to Yankee Stadium took a half hour with Manhattan traffic making it a rather long trip to the Bronx, but they arrived with plenty of time to take their seats directly behind the Yankees dugout on first base.

"Ohmigod," Adrianna gushed as they walked to their seats holding hot dogs, popcorn and beer. "These seats are to die for. And on the day of the game? How'd you manage it for the championship team?"

Dante's chest puffed out. "I told you I have connections." Thanks to his contact, the tickets were waiting for them at will call.

"This is going to be so much fun." The last game she'd been to was when her father as governor had thrown the first pitch and it had all been about image. He'd been all about the press and not about the family day he'd promised her, so it hadn't been much fun for her. She'd vowed to never come to a baseball game again. And she hadn't until now.

Dante turned to glance at her and realized just what a big kid Adrianna could be. He liked that she was so open and honest with her emotions. She wore her heart on her sleeve, which was why the fact that she'd been dating another man while sleeping with him ten years ago made no sense. How could *she* show him such affection, make love to him so passionately, and yet all the time be going behind his back with another man? It didn't make sense when her father had told him back then and didn't make sense now. She'd apologized for the past, but had never fully explained what happened.

Dante took a deep breath. He had to stop letting negative thoughts take over. Why let nagging doubts spoil their romantic day? "I'm glad you're enjoying the game," he said, taking a sip of beer from the large plastic cup. His questions would just have to wait for another time, but someday, someday soon, he'd want to know the answers.

Adrianna glanced sideways at Dante. "I guess it's easy to tell that I don't get out much, huh?"

"I think you've led a very sheltered life," Dante admitted.

"There wasn't much room for fun in the Wright household," Adrianna replied.

"True, but at least you didn't have to worry about whether a fight was going to break out on your floor," Dante said, thinking back to some rough patches at the orphanage. "Or if you might have to protect your boys. Or wonder if there was going to be enough food to go around in the dining hall."

"I'm sorry, Dante, I must sound extremely ungrateful for the life I had."

"And should I hate you because you had and I didn't?" He shook his head. "I've learned to make peace with the cards I was dealt. And trust me, it hasn't been easy. To never know where you truly come from…" Dante's voice trailed off and it gave Adrianna pause. He never talked about being abandoned as a child.

"Peanuts, peanuts!" A vendor stopped on the steps in front of them and displayed some to Adrianna, but she shook her head.

"It must be hard for you not knowing who your birth parents are."

"It's funny. As a child, I would look into strangers' faces wondering if they were my mom and dad. Trying to see if I could see any reflection of myself in them, but eventually I had to give up the ghost."

"Did you ever try to find them?"

Dante shook his head. "Why bother? My mother couldn't be bothered to take care of me as a toddler and abandoned me at a hospital. That's when it hit me. Would I really want to know that person? And the answer was no."

Adrianna's eyes teared up as she thought of Dante abandoned as a child with no one to turn to but the system. Thank God he'd lucked out and met Malik, Quentin and Sage.

"Is everything okay?" Dante asked. When she nodded,

he asked again. "Are you sure? I'm sorry, I didn't mean to bring you down talking about the past." He reached for his beer which he'd set on the concrete floor, but Adrianna placed a hand in his lap.

"Don't ever be sorry. You have every right to feel sad, ambivalent or just plain angry for the hand you were dealt in life. It was a raw deal and I'm sorry."

Dante leaned over and brushed his lips across hers. "Thank you, darling. So let's turn this dial back to some fun, all right?" He stood up and cheered. "C'mon, Yankees!"

Adrianna got in on the fun and shouted right along with him. Pretty soon the somber mood that had overtaken them had vanished and was replaced with good times.

After the game, Dante's friend helped them get access to the locker rooms. Dante and Adrianna waited outside until the players filed out. Thanks to Dante, Adrianna now had a Yankees baseball from the gift store signed by Dante's favorite player.

"I had a great time," Adrianna said as she snuggled in his arms on the drive back to the city.

"So did I," Dante replied. "I can't believe that last home run. The Yankees are a gifted team."

Once back at Dante's place, duty called and Adrianna used her cell phone to check on her father. Nigel indicated that her Aunt Mimi, Madison's mother, had dropped by for a visit which had tired him out, but he was now resting comfortably. Thank God for Nigel, Adrianna thought as she hung up. If it weren't for him, she wouldn't have the opportunity to spend this amount of time with Dante. She'd be tied to her father's bedside. The nurse she'd hired helped as well, but it was Nigel that her father relied on and respected.

"Everything okay?" Dante asked, coming into the living room with a gift-wrapped box with a large bow on it.

Adrianna's eyes grew wide. "Everything is fine and is that for me?" She pointed to the box.

Dante rubbed his goatee. "Hmm, let me think…of course it's for you, silly. Open it up." He plopped down on the couch beside her.

Slowly, Adrianna untied the bow and lifted the top lid. Inside lay a beautiful passion-colored one-shouldered draped dress. Adrianna grinned from ear to ear. "Dante, you shouldn't have."

"Well." He shrugged. "What else were you going to wear to dinner? I know my sweats are quite the fashion statement, so if you want to wear them again, they are all yours."

"Absolutely not," Adrianna said, taking the designer dress out of the box and dangling it over the side of the couch. "This dress is stunning and it must be worn."

"Ya think?" A glint of humor flickered in his eyes. "Go try it on."

"Gladly," Adrianna said, but instead of going to his bathroom to change, she unzipped her skinny jeans and slowly started to pull them down her hips. Surprisingly, she wasn't embarrassed at the prospect of undressing right in front of Dante. She loved the way he looked at her with such passion lurking in those brown depths.

Dante raised a brow. "Hmm…I'm getting my own private strip show. I like."

"Oh yes." Adrianna turned backward to Dante and peeled off her tunic inch by inch. She gave him a wink just as she pulled it over her head and tossed it to him. He caught it with one hand.

Dante was thrilled watching Adrianna undress.

She had such a beautiful body. She was all curves and lusciousness. Dante wanted to take her back to his bed and have his way with her, but there was plenty of time for that later. He had a quiet romantic dinner planned at the River Café that Adrianna was going to love.

Bare-chested, wearing only bikini panties, Adrianna felt no shame reaching for the dress. She slipped it over her head. When she was fully dressed she spun around, but Dante remained silent.

"Well?" She bunched her shoulders.

The hem of the dress hit Adrianna's gorgeously toned thighs and the satin draped over her sexy shoulders with ease. "Breathtaking," Dante whispered. He quickly rose to his feet, closed the distance between them and enveloped her in his arms. The kiss was electric.

Once they finally broke free, Dante said, "Now, I'm completely underdressed for dinner." He motioned down to his jersey and jeans.

"Then let's get showered." Adrianna smirked, heading toward the master bedroom.

An hour later, Adrianna emerged from the master bedroom wearing the dress along with the drop diamond earrings and matching necklace she'd worn the night before. Luckily, she had her compact with some pressed powder, lip liner and gloss in her cocktail purse. Her makeup was minimal, so she hoped Dante wasn't too disappointed.

He was waiting for her in the living room in a Calvin Klein black suit and a pink tie that matched her dress. "Someone looks dashing." Adrianna smiled as she approached him.

"And you look amazing as well."

"Do I?" Adrianna asked, fluffing her hair. "I don't have my makeup so forgive the bare face."

Dante stroked her cheek. "Don't you get it by now? You could be wearing absolutely nothing and you'd still look beautiful to me."

Adrianna brushed her lips across his. "Thank you. You make me feel like a million dollars."

"Let's go, baby."

Nestled under the Brooklyn Bridge, the River Café was every bit as romantic and elegant as Dante envisioned. It offered a sweeping view of the Manhattan skyline that Dante knew would appeal to Adrianna.

Holding hands, they walked the short pathway through the garden to the restaurant. They took time to stop and literally smell the roses. Then the hostess seated them in the Terrace Room at a table near the floor-to-ceiling window.

"This is a perfect ending to an amazing day," Adrianna commented after Dante ordered a bottle of Madeira wine from one of River Café's finest collections.

"I agree," Dante said. "It's been so long since I've taken a day off. For last few years, I've been a workaholic, devoting myself to building up Dante's and now Renaissance."

"That you haven't stopped to take time for yourself?" Adrianna asked. It reminded her of herself. She'd been so unhappy with her life that she'd wrapped herself up in her work, barely dating. She'd stopped living.

"Exactly. You know what I'm talking about."

"I do, but now we have so much more to look forward to," Adrianna said. "Can you believe we'll have our television show soon?"

Dante nodded. "I can hardly believe it, but it's the next

logical step for me. I've achieved the goal of owning my own restaurants and creating my visions. Now it's time to take it to a bigger audience."

The waiter returned with the Madeira wine and poured them each a glass. "Thank you," Dante said and took care of ordering the bay scallop ceviche as an appetizer.

"And you're sure you don't mind having me along for the ride?" Adrianna asked.

"Why would you ask me that?" Dante asked. "Are you still unsure of me?"

"No." Adrianna shook her head. "But maybe of myself."

"Don't doubt yourself." Dante reached for Adrianna's hand and squeezed it. "You have what it takes to be a great chef. I saw that at Renaissance when you pinch-hit for my staff. You have great instincts which is why our show is going to be a success." He reached for his wineglass. "So let's toast. To making it big."

"To making it big." Adrianna clinked her glass with his.

Dinner was a feast of the senses with crispy duck breast with white truffle honey and potato croquettes for Adrianna, and Mediterranean seabass with a chorizo and shrimp stuffing and zucchini for Dante. Afterward, they sat and listened to a band singing Frank Sinatra tunes.

Adrianna soaked in the ambience as this was the last night she could stay with Dante. She needed to get back to her father and spend time with him. No one knew how long he had left—months or even weeks—so she was going to have to enjoy this night with Dante because they might be few and far between from here on out.

So when Dante asked her to dance, she gladly accepted.

Time spent in his arms was like heaven. He clutched her to him and together they swayed to the soothing big band music.

When it was over, Dante took her back to his place and made love to her slowly, gently and with a reverence Adrianna had never felt before with any other man. Afterward as they lay snuggled together in each other's arms, Adrianna said, "This has been one of the best weekends I've had in a long time and I will cherish it."

"I feel the same way," Dante replied. "And there're many more in store." He lowered his head and captured her mouth in a long, deep kiss.

Chapter 8

"Are you nervous?" Malik asked Dante when they met at the gym for their weekly workout session. Before Malik was married, they used to go more often, but now they had settled on Wednesdays.

"About what?" Dante asked as he completed several reps on the chest press.

"Don't you start taping the show next week?" Malik inquired, grabbing two twenty-pound weights.

"We do, but I'm not too worried about it," Dante responded. "Adrianna and I already met with the show's producer on Monday and discussed the vision for the show. And in the interim, she and I have collaborated on several ideas for dishes, so I think we'll be fine." Over the weekend—in bed—they'd discussed ideas they had for dishes for the show.

Malik stopped lunging and lifting the free weights to stare at Dante. "You and Adrianna have collaborated?"

He raised a brow. "So I take it your relationship has been reignited?"

Dante laughed out loud. "C'mon, don't act like Sage didn't call you and spill the beans when she found out we'd be hosting the show together. I know Miss Thing told you."

"Actually, I didn't know," Malik replied, continuing with his lunges. "She'd left a couple of messages for me, but I've been so busy with another renovation at one of my community centers that I hadn't had the time to call her back."

"Well, now you know."

"And things are going well?" he asked, returning to his lunges while doing bicep curls.

"If by 'well,' you mean we're not arguing and have made up in bed, then the answer would be a resounding yes."

"That's great," Malik replied. "It's good to see you happy, man."

"I feel blessed," Dante said. "To have Adrianna in my life after all these years and to have my career taking off right now, life couldn't be better."

"You are glowing, girlfriend," Madison said when they met for manicures and pedicures at Madison's favorite salon that afternoon.

"Am I really?" Adrianna asked and glanced at her reflection in the mirror. "Here's my color." Adrianna handed the manicurist the nail color she'd selected.

"Clearly, some good loving is doing wonders for your complexion," Madison stated. "Care to pass some of it along to us sexually-repressed sistas?"

"Madison, you always have several guys on a string," Adrianna responded.

"And none of them have rocked my boat recently, but Dante must have all the right moves." Madison patted Adrianna's knee.

"Madison! Hush!" Adrianna colored and she turned around to see if anyone was listening to their conversation. "What if someone heard you?"

"What if they did?" Madison asked, raising her voice just an octave higher. "They're all probably wishing they were you."

Adrianna laughed and instantly relaxed. Trust Madison to give it to her straight.

"So, give me some juicy details."

"All I will say is that Dante and I have reconnected and the sparks—" Adrianna's eyes flew upward "—are just amazing. I don't remember ever feeling this way, even back then. Maybe I was just young and naive and didn't know true passion. But now… Whew." She snapped her fingers. "It's like every emotion has been heightened. Every kiss, every touch. Every time we're together it's like the Fourth of July."

"Wow!" Madison's eyes grew large. "That's fabulous, darling. See, what you needed all this time was for Dante to release the sexual diva within."

"He has," Adrianna replied. "I feel so much more in tune with myself and my feelings and my desires. It's been truly liberating."

"And trust me, now that the sexual diva is loose, you'll never want her back in."

"You're a hot mess, Madison." Adrianna chuckled.

"Are you as excited as I am?" Adrianna asked as the elevator climbed toward the tenth floor of Lawrence Enterprises where the television studio was located.

"I am." Dante squeezed her hand. "This is a dream come true."

They hadn't been able to spend the entire weekend together as Adrianna had to be with her father, but she had come to Manhattan on Saturday and they'd attended a street festival and spent the better part of the evening in bed.

When they arrived to the television studio floor, they released hands. They had decided to keep their relationship private from people other than their family. The world did not need to know they were an item. The production team was already in full setup mode when they arrived. Todd was there waiting for them.

"Dante." Todd shook his hand and then hers. "Adrianna."

"Hi, Todd." Adrianna beamed.

"Are you both ready to make some magic happen on screen?" Todd asked.

"We are indeed," Dante replied.

"Let's get you two kids to hair and makeup," Todd said. He led them to a small area set up with two director's chairs with their names on them in front of two lighted mirrors.

Dante glanced at Adrianna and winked. He could sense her nervousness. Surprisingly, he was calm. He'd waited his whole life for a moment like this. He relished the opportunity to show the world exactly the type of chef Dante Moore was. He'd toiled in the trenches for long enough. It was his moment to shine. And with Adrianna at his side, he couldn't fail.

Spending time with her the last week had been amazing. Being able to wake up in her arms was the best way to start out a day. He knew she wouldn't be able to do it for too much longer with her father's health declining.

She was going to have spend more time in the Hamptons with him, but that didn't matter to Dante because as soon as he saw her, as soon as they came together, the rest of the world ceased.

"I just going to put a little pancake on you," the makeup artist told Dante. "The cameras can be harsh."

Dante smiled back at her. "No problem." While the makeup artist worked on him, a barber came over to touch up his haircut and his goatee. Then it was on to wardrobe. Several button-down shirts, trousers and even some jeans hung on a rack for Dante to choose from.

As he was perusing the clothing, Todd came toward him. "How's it going?"

"Fine," Dante said. "These are some great designers." He was familiar with several of the collections.

"Well, we want you to look stylish and sophisticated, yet approachable. We want the audience out there to be able to relate to your style. That's why we chose casual wardrobes for both you and Adrianna."

"I'm pretty much happy with everything you have here," Dante said, selecting a blue button-down shirt and a pair of jeans.

"Great! I'll see you at taping. I'm going to check on Adrianna."

Across the way, Adrianna was getting her hair done. She'd purposely come in with it washed and straight so the hair stylist would have a blank canvas to work on. "I just love your hair," the stylist gushed. "It's so thick and full. Women would kill for this head of hair."

"Thank you," Adrianna said.

"If you don't mind, I would like to give you just a few more layers. You'll still have the length, but it would be a little bit more modern. Then we're going to use a flat iron so that the hair frames your face."

"I'm completely open to all your suggestions." Adrianna hadn't cut any significant length off her hair in years. She supposed it came from having been a society wife and having her hair tastefully pulled back in a bun or an updo. Even after the divorce, Adrianna hadn't made any changes. She'd been so happy to move on with her life that she'd settled for the mundane. Not anymore. She was going after what she wanted.

A half hour later, Adrianna shook her hair in the mirror. It still reached past her shoulders, but had layers that accentuated her round face and petite nose. She loved the makeover.

"How do I look?" Adrianna asked when Dante walked toward her.

"Beautiful as always," Dante said, grabbing her and giving her a playful spin.

The television studio set was much different than the demo Dante and Adrianna used previously. The new set had a very modern, elegant feel with black cabinets, granite countertops and stainless steel appliances.

The production team walked them through the blocking of the different steps in the lobster macaroni and cheese they would be preparing. They would work as a team to create the dish, while each gave a different cooking tip or snippet into their everyday lives.

"What we're looking for," Todd said to Dante, "is for you to be yourself. Talk to the camera as if you were talking to one of your friends. Engage. Engage. Engage."

Dante nodded.

Just as he was about to walk on set, Ian, Sage, Malik and Quentin showed up in the television studio.

"What are you all doing here?" he asked, looking back and forth at his family. He'd mentioned the taping during Sunday dinner, but hadn't expected them to show up.

"Did you think we'd miss your big debut?" Sage said. She knew Dante had asked her to stay out of his business, but she couldn't resist being there to share his big moment and once she'd told Quentin and Malik they were in agreement.

"Sage is right," Malik said. He'd even dressed up for the occasion by pulling his dreads back in a ponytail and wearing slacks and a polo shirt instead of his usual jeans and dashiki.

Quentin was no different. His bald head looked freshly shaven and he was wearing a pullover sweater and dark jeans. "We're not here to get in the way," Quentin began. "We're just here to support you."

Adrianna came up behind Dante and touched his shoulder. "You're lucky to have your family here, so enjoy it. Some of us are not so lucky."

"Oh, I'm not upset," Dante protested, smiling at his family. "Just happily surprised. Now step back so we can get to work."

"Break a leg." Sage gave him an enthusiastic thumbs-up.

"Thanks, kiddo."

"So are you ready to begin?" Todd asked, coming forward. "We are on a tight schedule." He glanced down at his watch.

"Absolutely," Adrianna and Dante said almost in unison.

"Ever the taskmaster," Ian commented from the

sidelines. "Let's go." He ushered Sage and the rest of the group to the back of the studio.

Dante and Adrianna walked on set and took their places.

"All right." The director gave the signal. "We're taping in one, two, three…"

"Welcome to *Easy Entertaining*. I'm Dante Moore."

"And I'm Adrianna Wright." Adrianna smiled at the camera.

"And we'll be showing you how to turn a simple meal into a knockout with your family and friends," Dante said, reading from the cue cards.

"Today, we'll be making lobster macaroni and cheese," Adrianna added. "It's a simple dish, but has lots and lots of flavor."

The taping continued smoothly with Adrianna focusing on chopping the shallots and garlic for the cheese base while Dante sautéed the shallots and garlic in some butter.

"Add some salt and ground black pepper for taste." Adrianna came over to the stove and added pinches of each to the pot. "Isn't that right, Dante?"

"That's perfect, Adrianna." Dante glanced at her. She was doing well and didn't seem nervous anymore. He knew she could do it because the kitchen was her element. "Then you add five tablespoons of flour as a thickening agent. What we're looking for here is a smooth texture in your cheese sauce," he said as he whisked the ingredients before adding white wine and heavy cream to the mix. After she'd boiled the pasta, Adrianna joined Dante and the stove, topping off his sauté with some paprika and cayenne pepper for seasoning.

"It's going to give your mac-and-cheese that extra

kick," Dante stated, jabbing his fists at the screen, "by adding a depth of flavor and earthiness."

They finished as a team by dicing up the lobster and shredding the sharp white cheddar and Gruyère cheese before adding them and the penne pasta to the sauce and placing it in a casserole dish.

"To give it texture, I'm going to add some panko bread crumbs and fresh parsley." Adrianna sprinkled both across the top of the casserole.

"Then you put it in the oven on three hundred fifty degrees," Dante said. "And voilà. Lobster macaroni and cheese. For my extended family, I've found that this recipe is sure to please even the most discerning palate for Sunday dinner."

When it was done, Dante took the casserole out of the oven and spooned some onto a small plate. Adrianna came over with two forks and they each took a bite.

"Hmm, delicious…" Dante stated, rolled his eyes upward. "This has just the right creaminess thanks to the different cheeses."

"And the right amount of spice thanks to the paprika and cayenne pepper seasoning," Adrianna responded.

"As you can see you don't have to be a chef to complete the recipes we'll be showing you on *Easy Entertaining*. All you need is a desire to cook and fresh ingredients," Dante concluded, and he and Adrianna both smiled broadly.

"And cut!" the director yelled.

"That was perfect," Ian said from the sidelines. "I knew I made the right decision when I hired you both. That taping was great."

"I couldn't agree more," Todd stated. "It had the right balance of naturalness while still giving cooking tips."

"It was better than perfect," Sage gushed as Dante

came off set. "You were magnificent." She rushed over to give Dante a hug. "I'm so proud of you."

"Yeah, man, you were great on camera," Quentin added. "And if you don't mind, I'd like to take a couple of shots of you in the kitchen." He held up his camera perched around his neck and glanced in Ian's direction for approval. "I would of course be willing to sell them to *CRAZE* for your promotion of the new show."

CRAZE was a lifestyle magazine that Lawrence Enterprises had launched last year and Quentin had already sold several photos to the publication.

"That sounds like a fine idea, Quentin. You have my permission." Ian nodded.

"Where would you like us?" Dante asked, including Adrianna in the "us." She was the second half of the team and he wasn't going to let his family exclude her because they weren't happy about their renewed relationship.

"Of course." Quentin nodded. He'd heard the tone in Dante's voice and knew he didn't appreciate the exclusion even if it was an oversight on his part. "Let's take some test shots behind the counter."

"No problem." Dante and Adrianna returned to the set.

Quentin took several shots of the pair in front of the counter and near the stove. "Think I've got it," he said after a short while. "You're both naturally photogenic. The camera loves you."

"I'm banking on that," Ian said.

"How about we go celebrate?" Malik spoke up. "It's not every day our brother becomes a household name."

Dante laughed at the pronouncement. "I'm not there yet."

"But you will be," Malik returned.

"That sounds like a fine idea," Sage replied.

"How about my place?" Quentin suggested.

"Does Avery even cook?" Dante inquired.

"Very funny." Quentin chuckled. "We can order in. Would 6:00 p.m. work for everyone?"

"Fine with me. See you all there," Sage and Malik agreed on their way out.

After everyone had left, Adrianna and Dante hung back on set. They were both quiet, silently soaking up the moment.

"That was pretty amazing, wasn't it?" Dante finally said after several long minutes.

"It was." Adrianna hadn't felt nervous at all because as soon as she glanced over at those compelling brown eyes or the confident set of Dante's shoulders, she'd eased and breezed through the taping.

"I couldn't have done it without you." Dante brought her hand up to his and kissed it and released it quickly before anyone saw him. "And wouldn't want to."

In just a short time, the feelings he'd felt for Adrianna had been resurrected. He was trying to push them down because his mind cautioned him to take things slowly. He'd risked his heart with her before and nearly lost his soul forever.

"Me, too." Her eyes were bordered with tears.

Chapter 9

When Dante and Adrianna made it to Quentin and Avery's town house on the Upper East Side, the celebration was already in full swing. Sage, Quentin, Avery, Malik and Peyton were already there.

As he walked in, Dante was still surprised that Quentin had chucked his loft for a town house, but he guessed that's what happened when a man got married and started a family. His priorities changed. Dante wanted the same one day. He didn't know if that would happen with Adrianna or with someone else but he wanted a family. He wanted someone to love him unconditionally, for better for worse and who wouldn't leave.

The town house was elegantly decorated with Avery's touch in classic muted tones, but yet had Quentin's flare. His colorful photographs were remarkably decorated throughout the downstairs and gave the décor punch.

Several bottles of champagne and glasses were already

set out on the dining-room glass table. The dining-room set was classic black-and-white and it looked like several of his favorite appetizers from Dante's were on display for the family to nibble on.

"Did Sage call you to arrange this?" Dante asked Avery as she carefully arranged each platter on the table. She was a perfectionist very much like him.

"Who else?" Avery asked.

Dante shook his head. Sage certainly knew how to take charge. It was one of the many things he loved about her. Dante strolled over to give Sage a kiss on the cheek. "Thank you, my dear."

"For what?"

"For getting all my favorite food here." He motioned to the table.

"You're welcome." She gave him a pat on the behind. "Don't you know I'd do anything for you?"

"I do. Where's Ian?" Dante asked, glancing around.

"He's running a little behind, but he'll be here."

"To the man of the hour." Malik came forward to give Dante a flute of champagne.

Malik noticed Adrianna standing alone by the dining-room doorway. She looked uneasy in a roomful of people, some of which she'd once called friends, so he handed her a glass of champagne. "And to the lady of the hour."

"Thank you, Malik." Adrianna smiled as she accepted the glass with shaking fingers. She hadn't been nervous during the taping of the show that had been a walk in the park compared to this. Being around Dante's family who were clearly ambivalent about her presence in his life was disconcerting. If she left, no one would probably even notice.

"They did a fabulous job, baby." Quentin squeezed his svelte wife, Avery, as he came to her side. After a few short months, she'd already lost all her baby weight. "You should have seen them. They made cooking in front of a bunch of cameras seem effortless."

"Well, what can I say?" Dante leaned back. "I have a gift."

"Oh, someone's getting a big head now." Adrianna chuckled from the sidelines.

"He deserves it," Sage pronounced, channeling her gaze in Adrianna's direction. "He's worked hard for everything he's earned."

The group suddenly became silent at the implication that Adrianna had not had to work for the opportunity she'd earned.

Despite Sage's comment, Adrianna maintained a stiff upper lip for the rest of the evening. She stayed close to Dante's side, nibbling on appetizers and drinking champagne, but she was never fully comfortable.

The situation became much worse when Avery brought out her three-month-old baby girl, Bella.

"How's my goddaughter?" Dante asked, taking Bella from Avery's arms and holding the infant in the crook of his arm. He just loved holding the little girl. Whenever he held her he felt hope for the future and knew that anything was possible.

"She's beautiful, isn't she?" Avery asked, turning to Adrianna. Like any new mother, she was absolutely biased where her daughter was concerned.

Avery looked up and noticed the grief-stricken look on Adrianna's face. "Are you okay?" Avery asked.

Adrianna shook her head, unable to speak. Just seeing the baby brought up all the old emotions, all the guilt she felt at losing her and Dante's child. They should have had a little boy or girl of their own with Dante's light brown eyes and her smile, but because of her lies that precious gift had been taken away and she'd never fully recovered from the loss.

Adrianna watched Dante coo and make baby noises at Bella and felt a tug of guilt so strong she had to look away. She couldn't let him see how deeply affected she was.

As if she sensed her weakness from across the room, Sage focused on Adrianna's response to Bella and commented, "Do you have a problem with babies?"

Dante glowered at her. "Why would you ask something like that? Of course Adrianna doesn't have a problem with little Bella here." Dante took Bella's tiny hand in his and watched the infant grab hold of one of his fingers.

Adrianna watched the pure joy that crossed Dante's face at just holding his goddaughter. She could only imagine how he would have been as a father. He would have been warm and loving and completely unlike her own father, but she'd denied him that chance. "Excuse me, something is in my eye." Adrianna lowered her head. "Where's the powder room?"

"Down the hall and to the left," Avery offered and Adrianna quickly rushed off.

"Sage!" Dante whispered and Sage mouthed "What?"

"I'll go," Avery said and headed toward the powder room.

Dante pointed a finger at Sage for her to come toward him. He couldn't believe how insensitive she was being. "I warned you."

"I only asked if she had a problem with babies. What's her deal?"

"Don't be mad at Sage." Quentin stepped forward to her defense. "You know she can't help herself."

"Well, she should try harder," Dante said, bouncing

baby Bella in his arms. "Adrianna is a permanent fixture in my life for the immediate future."

"I realize that," Sage returned. "But forgive me if I'm a little bit apprehensive of Adrianna's intentions toward you."

"I thank you for caring, but enough with the warnings. I've been taking care of myself for a long time now."

"Yeah, you have," Quentin replied. "But we've always had each other's backs. It took you a long time to recover from Adrianna's deception before and we just want to make sure it doesn't happen again."

"No one can predict the future."

"No, we can't," Sage added, "but we can caution you when you're walking in front of a speeding train...to hang back. Did you see how she reacted around Bella?" Sage nodded to his goddaughter. "She was visibly shaken. Why is that? What is she hiding?"

"Sage, trust me." Dante glanced at the doorway. "I have some reservations, but I can't live my life in fear of what might happen. I just have to live life."

Quentin nodded. "I hear you."

"Sage, you're just going to have to accept that I know what's best for me and your behavior toward Adrianna can't continue."

"Fine." Sage folded her arms across her chest. Her gut instinct as a lawyer told her that something was off with Adrianna. She had intended to find out sooner, but had gotten too caught up with one of her cases, but there was no better time than the present to find out exactly what Adrianna was trying to hide. Sage stepped away privately to call the detective her firm kept on retainer. Patrick Kelly picked up on the second ring. "Patrick, I need you to do me a favor."

* * *

"Are you okay?" Avery asked Adrianna from the other side of the powder-room door.

"I'm fine."

"No, you're not. Sage wasn't too nice," Avery responded.

On the other side of the door, Adrianna blotted her eyes with a tissue from her purse. "No kidding."

"Please open the door, Adrianna. I'd like to talk to you."

Adrianna glanced at her reflection in the mirror. She looked a wreck. Her cheeks were stained red and her eyes were slightly puffy from crying. She took a deep breath and slowly opened the door.

Avery grabbed her hand. "C'mon, let's go to the kitchen. It'll be quiet there." Adrianna followed behind her, but stopped at the doorway.

"Why are you being nice to me?" Was she just trying to reel her in so she could throw her back to the sharks?

"Because…I know how hard the gang can be on outsiders," Avery responded, leaning against the island in the center of the kitchen. "Trust me, I know. When I had a difference of opinion with Malik about my biological father, it nearly destroyed his and Quentin's relationship, which I never, ever wanted. So, it wasn't smooth sailing for me, either, but somehow you've got to find a way to make peace with them."

"How do I do that?" Adrianna asked, pacing the floor as she wrung her hands. "They hate me."

"They don't hate you," Avery replied. "They don't trust you. There's a difference."

Adrianna rolled her eyes. "You could have fooled me."

"Take my advice," Avery said. "The best thing you

can do to prove them wrong is show them just how much you love Dante. The rest will fall into place."

Love Dante? Heck, she'd loved Dante her entire adulthood—that wasn't the problem. It was the lies she'd told that could come back to haunt her that threatened to destroy what they had. Just seeing Bella today had proven that. "You make it sound so easy."

"It is." Avery flashed a smile. "I had a rocky start with this family, too, but eventually they accepted me and they will accept you *in time*."

Adrianna touched her arm. "Thank you, Avery."

"You're welcome."

When she returned to the party, all eyes were on Adrianna and she felt like a deer in the headlights. Sage was the first to approach her.

"Listen, I'm sorry," Sage said. She could feel Dante's eyes burning a hole in the back of her head. She didn't want to be at odds with him, especially over Adrianna, so she would do whatever was necessary to prove she could be civil. "I was unforgivably rude and I apologize."

Adrianna glanced over at Dante and could feel the tension emanating from his every pore from across the room. He wanted her to get along with Sage so she would make an effort. "Apology accepted, Sage." She forced a smile.

"Thank you, you're very generous." Sage wasn't sure she would have reacted the same.

"And believe me when I say that I have no intention of hurting Dante again. I care a great deal about him."

"Glad to hear that because I will be watching you," Sage said and headed over to the bar to pour herself a drink.

Adrianna had no doubt Sage would be eyeing her like

a hawk. She had to pull herself together and not allow Sage to see just how baby Bella was affecting her.

Dante walked over to Adrianna with Bella still in his arms. "You okay?" he asked, giving her the once-over.

"Your family is a tough bunch to impress." Adrianna inhaled deeply.

"They are, so I appreciate the effort you're making," Dante said.

"I can't much blame them," Adrianna whispered. "I hurt you once and they don't want to see that happen again. How can I be upset with them for wanting to protect you?"

"That may be true, but Sage still has no right to be rude to you."

"I'm a tough cookie," Adrianna replied. "You don't have to worry about me."

"Do you want to hold her?" Dante asked. He was sure Sage was wrong about Adrianna. She'd always wanted children in the past and he couldn't imagine that wanting a family now would be the one thing they didn't share in common.

Adrianna shook her head. "I wouldn't know how." She didn't think she could bear to hold the little girl in her arms.

"It's easy." Dante slowly eased the baby into her arms.

Adrianna looked down and was amazed at the lovely creation Quentin and Avery had made together. Bella was a testament of their love for each other. Her eyes misted with tears as she walked over to Avery and handed her daughter to her. "She's beautiful. You're truly lucky."

Dante and Adrianna didn't stay too much longer at Quentin's after that and said their good-byes, much to Adrianna's delight.

"So, where to?" Dante said. He hoped she would say his place. He was getting used to sleeping next to her.

It had been an emotional day and the only place Adrianna wanted to be was home. "Do you mind dropping me off in the Hamptons? I want to check on my father."

"Of course not." Dante was disappointed, but he tried not to show it.

"I'm sorry, but I really haven't spent enough time with him."

"I understand." He notified the driver and away they went.

Dante noticed Adrianna was withdrawn and sullen on the drive to the Hamptons. There was a huge gap between them and she sat facing the window. Dante knew it had to do with Sage's behavior toward her.

"Adrianna." He scooted closer to her. "I'm sorry about Sage. I've warned her that I'm not going to take any more of her shenanigans."

"It's not just Sage," Adrianna said. "Your entire family doesn't want you to be with me. It's hard to fight that." From the moment they met, it seemed like everyone and everything was against them. First her father and now Dante's family. "Maybe we're just not meant to be."

Dante grabbed her chin and forced her to face him. "I don't believe that. We've just found each other again and I'm not going to let anyone get in the way of that ever again. Promise me you won't, either."

She gave a reluctant smile. "I promise."

The way Dante said it with such conviction made Adrianna believe it, too.

Chapter 10

Dante and Adrianna taped half a dozen episodes of *Easy Entertaining* over the next several weeks. Some of the recipes were simple, like the lobster macaroni and cheese, and others were more complicated, like coq au vin or cassoulet. Due to her father's failing health, Adrianna had taken a leave of absence as a *Foodies* magazine reviewer, so she could spend more time with him and Dante.

When they weren't in the studio taping, Dante and Adrianna spent as much time together as possible, whether it was cooking at Dante's, in-line skating in Central Park or just snuggled underneath a blanket watching a movie. Dante couldn't remember the last time he'd felt this happy, this content.

He didn't care when Todd summoned them to review episodes back in the Lawrence Enterprises control room and noted items that they needed to work on because the easy rapport they shared and natural chemistry showed on-screen and off.

"These are really good, but there is still room for improvement," Todd commented. "Adrianna, I need you to chime in more about your life experiences and cooking tips."

Adrianna nodded.

"Dante, you've got cooking in front of the camera down pat. Occasionally, you forget to look up. We need the viewers to connect with you as a food authority."

"Thanks, Todd. I appreciate all your comments, good or bad," Dante replied.

"Ian and I think you are both doing an incredible job and we'll be proceeding to the next phase, publicity. Mr. Davis took some excellent working photos of you at your first show. Now we'll be having our photographer take publicity shots of you that will appear in the magazines, billboards and advertisements promoting the show. Then you'll do some interviews for *CRAZE*, radio and one of the local morning shows here in New York."

"Sounds great," Adrianna responded. "When do we get started?"

"How does now sound?" Todd replied. "I have you signed up for a photo session in our studio downstairs, so you had better get going."

With hair and makeup, the photo shoot lasted over two hours, but the photographer got some great shots of them.

"Our faces are going to be on billboards across New York," Adrianna said excitedly. "Can you believe it?"

"Time is moving quickly," Dante responded. "According to Todd, WTTG intends on premiering *Easy Entertaining* in a couple of weeks. Malik was right. Pretty soon we'll be household names."

"From your lips to God's ears," Adrianna replied.

* * *

Sage put down the phone receiver. She had all the ammunition she needed. Patrick, her detective, had found out the secret Adrianna had been carrying and perhaps the reason she hadn't returned to New York before now. Adrianna had married her ex and suffered a miscarriage, four months into their marriage. If Dante ever found out that she'd been sleeping with another man while seeing him, it would devastate him.

Was that why she'd stayed away so long, so the memories would dissipate and she could finally face him? Sage wondered if should tell Dante the truth. He had a right to know. Yet on the other hand, he might not appreciate her meddling. Sage was conflicted, so she called Quentin and Malik for advice and asked them to meet her at Dante's. She'd called ahead and Dante was still at Renaissance.

"So what do you think I should do?" Sage asked after she'd ordered them a round of drinks.

"Stay out of it," Quentin stated.

"I agree. It's not your place to tell him," Malik added. "It's up to Adrianna to tell Dante what happened back then."

"Don't you think I should call her out on it?" Sage asked.

"Absolutely not." Quentin shook his head. "It's just like you to be combative and in-your-face. But you have to stay out of this, you hear me?"

"Think about what putting yourself in the middle could do to your relationship with Dante," Malik added. "He might not ever forgive you for meddling. Would it really be worth it just to say 'I told you so'?"

Sage rolled her eyes. She hated when they were right, but they were. She had no place in Dante's business. He was a grown man and had to learn from his mistakes just as she had when he, Malik and Quentin had warned her away from Ian. Dante would have to learn Adrianna's secret from the lady herself. He would never hear it from Sage's lips.

Just then, Dante walked through the doors of his tapas restaurant. "What are you guys doing here? Did I miss a happy hour notice?" he asked.

"Well, someone's been so busy these days that we hardly get to see you anymore." Sage pouted, noting the suspicious lines at the corner of Dante's mouth.

"Oh, c'mon, I fail to cook *one* Sunday dinner and I'm being roasted over the coals?" Adrianna had tickets to a Broadway show she'd been dying to see and he didn't have the heart to say no.

"We understand, man," Malik said. "When we first got together, Peyton and I were hot and heavy so much we shut out the world. So I ain't going to hate on you getting some luvin'."

"I hear you." Quentin gave Malik some dap.

"Getting close to Adrianna again has completely floored me, guys," Dante said, scooting a stool underneath him. His bartender immediately came over and slid a bottle of beer his way. "Thanks, Mike."

"Are you saying you've fallen in love with Adrianna again?" Sage inquired.

Dante nodded. "I think I have. I certainly haven't felt this way in a long time."

"Since the first time you were together?" Quentin offered.

"So it's gotten serious between you two?" Malik asked.

"I can definitely see a future with Adrianna."

Sage nearly choked on the apple martini she was drinking and Quentin had to pat her back.

Dante glanced in her direction. "You okay?" He doubted she was too happy to hear those words come out of his mouth, but they were true. He was falling in love with Adrianna.

"Oh, I'm fine," she said even though she really wasn't. She hated to keep vital information from Dante, but she couldn't interfere, especially now that he was back in love with the woman.

"Good," Dante replied. "Because who knows? There might be a new addition to our clan real soon."

"I'm sorry, Adrianna, but your father isn't getting any better. I'm afraid his health is going to deteriorate rapidly from here on out," Howard's physician had stated in mid-June.

"Isn't there anything more you can do, Doctor Baker?" Adrianna had asked. She was spending as much time as possible with her father while still balancing her career and budding relationship with Dante.

"Adrianna, I wish there were," Dr. Baker replied, "but your father has stage four colon cancer. Nothing more can be done except to make him feel more comfortable."

"So I'm just supposed to watch him die?" Adrianna murmured.

"You have to be strong," Dr. Baker had replied. "If your father sees you fall apart, it will only make him hurt worse. Remember, stiff upper lip."

Stiff upper lip. Those words resonated throughout the morning in Adrianna's mind. Isn't that what her father always said even when the tabloids or papers would come after him as governor? So what if the press was calling her father names. *Don't bow down to their level,* her mother would add.

And when the time came for her to marry Phillip, her

father had walked into the church where she was getting dressed and told her again to have a stiff upper lip. "What you're doing is best for your child," he'd said. "Remember that." She was so used to holding things inside that she was uncertain if losing her father was supposed to be any different. He was the only family she had left and he was dying.

"Ms. Adrianna, are you okay?" Nigel asked when he found her sobbing in the study.

Adrianna wiped the tears away with the back of her hand and blinked several times. "I'm fine, Nigel," Adrianna said, turning around. "Is Father okay?"

"Yes, he has been sleeping soundly since Dr. Baker gave him some morphine. Is there anything I can do for you?" Nigel inquired.

"No."

"Do you need me to call Mr. Moore?" Nigel asked. He knew how important the young man was to her.

Adrianna shook her head adamantly. "No, that's not necessary." Why would Dante want to come and comfort her when her father was the man who had kept them apart a decade ago?

"As you wish," Nigel said and quietly left the room.

Adrianna walked over to the bookcase and pulled out several photo albums. There were pictures of them as a family when her mother was alive. There were photos of her dad on the campaign trail. And who was always by his side? Her and her mother. In some of the photos you could see the bored look on her face because they were always trotted out when it served his purpose.

Then she came across a few family vacation photos. She especially enjoyed seeing the trip to Jamaica. It was one of the rare moments when her father had let his guard down. The photo showed the two of them in the air parasailing. Her mother had been scared to death, but what fun it had been. Despite herself, she felt tears start to trickle down her face. She was reaching for a tissue when she felt someone's presence behind her.

When she looked up, Dante was standing in the study. Tears blinded her eyes and her voice was hoarse. "Wh-what are you doing here?"

"Nigel called me. He said you needed me. Is everything okay?"

Adrianna shook her hand and rushed into Dante's arms. "No," she cried, "my father is dying, Dante, and there's not a thing anyone can do."

"I'm sorry, baby." Dante hugged her tighter as sobs began to wrack her body. He stroked her hair, trying to calm her.

When she quieted, Dante helped her to the sofa near the window. "Did something else happen today to make you so upset?"

"Nothing more than usual," Adrianna answered. "Except I guess this time I finally heard the doctor. There is no hope for recovery. My father is terminal. And once he's gone I'll be all alone." She still would have her cousin Madison and Aunt Mimi, but her immediate family would be gone.

"I'm truly sorry, Adrianna. It must be difficult knowing the end is coming. But you must know that whatever happens you are not alone."

"I know that in here." Adrianna pointed to her head. "I just feel so powerless." She sat up and wiped her eyes. "The only thing I can do is make him comfortable and spend time with him, but you know what?"

"What?"

"I feel like a fake," Adrianna spat. "My father and I

haven't been close in years. It seems so disingenuous to act crestfallen now in his final days."

"He's still your father."

Adrianna turned and stared at Dante, shocked that he was even taking up for the man. "How can you stand up for him after everything he did to keep us apart all those years ago?"

"Because what's done is done, Adrianna. We can't go back and change the past. We just have to accept it."

"That's very magnanimous of you."

"I don't wish the man ill, Adrianna. He's a part of you and seeing how much this is hurting you, hurts me."

Adrianna rose from the couch and kneeled down to grab his large masculine hand in hers. "I am so lucky to have found you again," Adrianna said. "I truly don't deserve you."

Dante frowned. He reached out and bracketed her face in the palm of his hands. He probed her eyes for a moment. "Why would you say something like that? You absolutely deserve happiness now even more than ever."

Adrianna lowered her head to his lap. "I'm so glad to have you in my life."

"And I'll always be here."

Adrianna certainly hoped so because if the secret she'd been carrying ever came out and she lost Dante it would destroy her.

To cheer Adrianna up, Dante invited her to a charity gala at the Carlyle the following Saturday. Malik's organization, the Children's Aid Network, was hosting the event to raise funds for their community centers. Dante was hoping a night away from her father would be just the ticket to help Adrianna relax.

This time Adrianna drove herself into the city and met Dante at his condo as she intended to drive herself back that evening. They would only spend one night together, but every minute spent with him was thrilling.

She arrived simply dressed, wearing a tea-length chiffon dress with beaded halter straps accompanied by a clutch purse. Her hair was pulled back in a loose side ponytail.

"Are you ready for a fun night?" Dante asked. He looked spectacular in a black Italian crafted two-button suit and white tuxedo shirt.

"Oh yes." Adrianna sighed. "I've been looking forward to it all week."

When they arrived to the gala, Malik was standing outside the ballroom with Peyton. He looked dapper in a white tuxedo and his very pregnant wife, Peyton, wore a one-shouldered draped purple sheath.

"Peyton, you're looking lovely tonight," Dante commented, giving her a hug.

"Oh, you are too kind," Peyton said, rubbing her growing belly.

Adrianna kissed both of her cheeks. "He's right. You're glowing." Peyton's mocha-colored skin shone brightly.

Peyton beamed. "Thank you."

"How about a dance?" Dante asked Adrianna. A little fun on the dance floor would keep her mind off her father back home.

"Tango?" Adrianna winked.

"Absolutely, but hold on a sec."

Adrianna watched Dante rush over to the band and whisper something to them before he returned to her side and offered her his arm. "My lady."

Strands of "Assassin's Tango" began to play just

as Dante took her right hand in his. Soon they were stalking across the dance floor in slow, slow, quick, quick movements. Adrianna remembered to turn her shoulders slightly as Dante did when they reached the promenade.

Dante walked her forward, swiveled around and then slowly rocked her back and forth before turning her sharply toward him. Adrianna didn't realize she was laughing until Dante smiled at her. Getting out of the house was exactly what the doctor ordered.

When the dance ended, they returned to find Malik and Peyton smiling at them from the sidelines. "Wow, that was incredible," Peyton gushed. "I would love to be able to tango, but with this belly there's no way we could get that close."

Everyone chuckled.

"In due time, Peyton," Dante responded. "In due time."

"Dante." Malik patted him on the shoulder. "I'd love you to meet one of CAN's benefactors. I was telling him what a great chef you are and he's dying to have you cater our next charity event. Would you ladies mind if we steal him away for a minute?"

"Of course not," Adrianna responded. It was nice to see Dante's family finally warming up to her.

Malik introduced Dante to Arthur Rutherford, a huge charity activist and considered among the New York elite. "Mr. Moore, I hear great things about you," Arthur replied, shaking Dante's hand.

"Thank you. It's a pleasure to meet you, sir. The work you've done for the Children's Aid Network is great. Like Malik, I grew up in an orphanage and know how important it is once you succeed to give back, which is why I'm willing to donate my catering services free of charge at the next Children's Aid Network event."

Arthur was shocked. "That's an incredible offer, Mr. Moore. To have a chef of your caliber and a soon-to-be television star will be a big draw to our next event."

Dante glanced in Malik's direction. "Yeah, I've been talking you up," Malik offered at his side. "You're looking at the next Emeril."

"Well, I for one am looking forward to sampling your food," Arthur said.

"Thank you," Dante replied. "But I won't be the only one on the television show. I have an amazingly beautiful cohost, Adrianna Wright." Dante turned and looked around but she was nowhere in sight. "Just you wait, she's a star."

Adrianna was staring out the window when Dante came up behind her and wrapped his arms around her midsection. She'd had to get away from Peyton, not that Malik's wife had done anything wrong. The problem was everywhere she went she was confronted with babies. First she had a meltdown when she saw Dante holding Bella and now seeing Peyton pregnant… It reminded her of when she'd been pregnant.

It was getting harder and harder to keep the truth from Dante. She'd fallen deeper in love with him than the first time they'd been together, which is why telling him the truth now would hurt so much. But how could she not? How could she continue to have this secret hanging over their relationship? If she didn't tell him now, she would never be truly free to enjoy him.

"Hey, you." She turned around and gave him a quick kiss.

"How'd it go?"

"Looks like I have another catering event lined

up," Dante said. "I even offered my services free of charge."

"You are so generous," Adrianna said. "It's one of the things I love about you." Once she said the word *love* out loud, she realized it was out there and she couldn't take it back. So she added, "Like your sense of spontaneity and getting us tickets to the Yankees game."

"You don't have to cover up how you feel, Adrianna," Dante responded, looking at her intently. "Because I love you, too."

"You do?" Adrianna's eyes grew wide and her eyes misted with tears.

"Yes," he stated emphatically as he looked longingly into her eyes. "Can't you see it by now? I'm crazy about you."

"Oh, Dante." Adrianna swung her arms around his neck and pulled him into a sensuous embrace. She didn't care that she was in the middle of a crowded room. The man she loved just said he loved her back and she was over the moon.

Her lips sparked to life the instant they made contact with Dante's. His tongue coaxed and teased a response from her like an expert craftsman until she was fully aware and ready for him.

"Let's get out of here," Dante groaned and grabbed her hand.

They'd nearly made it out the door when Malik stopped them on the way out. "Are you guys sneaking out?" he inquired.

"Absolutely," Dante said. "The lady and I have some urgent plans." His eyes scrutinized Adrianna from head to toe.

"Then don't let me stand in your way." Malik stepped aside. "If I could leave discreetly, trust me, I would, but luckily I have a pregnant wife which gives me an easy excuse. Have a great night." Malik gave Dante a wink.

"Oh, we will."

Half an hour later, Dante was pressing Adrianna against his bedroom door and ravishing her with his mouth while his hands had their way with her. She responded to him with a burst of passion that staggered but didn't deter him. His lips deserted hers for a moment to nibble at her earlobe and his hands curved possessively over the swell of her soft behind. Adrianna didn't know where Dante would touch or kiss her next and it excited her to no end.

Dante wanted more than just kissing. He wanted to taste every part of her. With lightning speed, he wrapped his arms around her waist and scooped her off her feet to carry her to the bedroom.

He laid her on the bed, but Adrianna sat up and together they divested each other of every ounce of clothing. As if on their own accord, her hands reached up, wrapped her arms around his neck and pulled him down on top of her.

"Make love to me, make me yours," Adrianna murmured.

He parted her lips with the tip of his tongue and she opened completely for him. She took his tongue into her mouth, savored it and exulted in it. Dante had his own style of kissing that made her completely his. He fondled one breast with the palm of his hand before moving over to the next. Her breasts surged at the intimacy of Dante's touch. She wanted more.

When his hands slid across her flat stomach to gently caress her hips and her thighs, she trembled underneath him. It was when his fingers slipped inside her that she became nearly unglued. She lay panting; her chest heaving as his hands worked their magic and made love to her while his mouth drove her to the brink.

"Your body is so beautiful." Dante whispered his love for every part of her body as his hands skimmed the length of her back, bringing her closer to his hard body. They were so close. Flesh against flesh, man against woman. Dante could hear his heart hammering in his chest and the blood surging to the lower half of his body. He needed release.

As quickly as he could he protected them before slowly spreading her thighs and entering her. He sealed their bodies, binding them as one. Adrianna's body expanded to accommodate him as he began moving inside her. She wrapped her legs around his waist, drawing him deeper and deeper inside her body. Her breathing became faster as tension mounted so he quickened the pace and thrust his tongue into her mouth. When he withdrew slightly, Adrianna let out a whimper, so he plunged deeper again.

She lifted her hips to meet his every thrust. When his hardened tip grazed her womanly curve again, a moan escaped her lips, her legs began to quake and her muscles spasmed as she climaxed beneath him. Taut lines etched across his face as he, too, sped toward an overwhelming climax. When a tidal wave overtook him, Dante's entire body exploded racking him with pure pleasure.

Afterward, he held her tight in his arms. The heavy beating of his heart matched Adrianna. What they had just shared had been so incredible that Dante couldn't resist repeating the sentiment he'd said earlier at the charity event.

"I love you, Adrianna. I have never stopped," Dante said, lying in bed with her. "Even when I was angry with you, I loved you."

"I love you, too," Adrianna responded softly.

"I didn't think it was possible that I would ever find love again after I lost you," Dante admitted. "But I'm sure glad I did."

"Dante, about before…" Adrianna started. "There's so much history between us, so much left unsaid that I want to clear the air."

Dante shook his head. Those nagging questions he'd had before had vanished and now he just wanted to focus on the future. "I don't want to think about the past anymore, Adrianna, because it doesn't matter to me. Whatever happened back then I just want to put it behind us. I don't want to waste any more time."

"I know, but…"

"No buts." Dante shushed her with a kiss. "I just want to enjoy us, enjoy this." He gently pulled her into his arms and kissed her passionately until the wee hours of the morning.

Chapter 11

The aftershock of their declaration of love was even more potent in the daylight. Dante had given her a free pass last night from ever revealing the truth about why she'd married another man. But the weight of the guilt was still wearing heavily on her shoulders when Madison stopped by the house that Sunday.

"Hey." Madison gave her cousin a hug as she came through the front door. "How are you, darling? I was worried. I heard from Mama that Uncle Howard isn't doing too good."

"I'm hanging in there," Adrianna said, "but Father…" Her voice broke.

Madison touched her arm. "The end is near, isn't it?"

Adrianna nodded her head. "He's gotten weaker, so much so that he can barely sit up or feed himself. The hospice nurse is now here 24/7 because Nigel and I just can't do it alone anymore. His condition seemed to deteriorate almost overnight."

"What can I do?" Madison asked.

"Just your coming here means a lot." Adrianna reached for her hand and gave a gentle squeeze.

Madison smiled warmly. "I'm glad you said that." She reached behind her and pulled out a bag. "Because I'm staying overnight!" She slammed the front door.

"Oh, Maddie," Adrianna cried, "you have no idea how much I needed this."

"C'mon, girlfriend," Madison wrapped her arm around her cousin's waist. "Let's talk."

Over a big pot of tea with oatmeal raisin cookies, Adrianna's favorite that Nigel just so happened to have cooling, she and Madison caught up about what had happened over the past two months.

"You know, I was starting to think you were just a figment of my imagination," Madison started. "You've been back for nearly three months, but I have barely seen you. Then lo and behold I'm driving down Times Square and I see a huge billboard and an advertisement for you and Dante's *Easy Entertaining* show. You could have knocked me over with a feather."

"That's been the bright spot in the midst of all this misery," Adrianna said, taking a sip of tea and curling her legs underneath her. "Taping the show has been great. I think it's going to be a huge success."

"Of course it is," Madison returned, reaching for a cookie. "It has you. So…how's everything between you and Dante?"

Madison's eyes never left hers, so Adrianna couldn't lie and a broad smile spread across her face. "Dante told me he loves me last night."

"Are you kidding?" Madison kicked off her Manolo Blahnik heels and made herself comfortable on the couch.

"No, I'm not." Adrianna beamed. "He told me he'd always loved me."

"And…"

"And I told him I love him back."

"Girl, I am so thrilled for you," Madison said. "After all these years, to finally have your heart's desire? You must be on cloud nine."

"I am."

Madison sat back and studied her cousin's face. "Why do I hear some hesitancy in your voice?"

"There's not…" Adrianna began, but at Madison's raised brow, she stopped. "Okay, I do feel a little guilty."

"Why? You love him and he loves you. What else is there?"

"The real reason I left him ten years ago," Adrianna responded. "I feel like it's hanging over my head."

"Then you should tell him," Madison said matter-of-factly.

"I tried, but he wouldn't let me. He told me the past wasn't important anymore and that I should let it go."

"Then let it go. He's given you an out. Take it."

"I'm not sure I can."

"Why do you want to tell him so much? You say it's because he has the right to know, but it sounds like to me it's more about clearing your own conscience and making you feel better. Because I doubt hearing the truth will make Dante feel good."

"Wow!" Madison's words stung, but were true. Was she doing this more for herself than for Dante?

"All I'm saying is give this some thought before you go torch what you and Dante have just built together because you're feeling guilty."

Adrianna nodded. "I will certainly think long and hard before I make any decisions."

* * *

On Monday morning, Dante paced the floor of the television studio and glanced down at his watch. He was already dressed and in makeup, but Adrianna was late which was unlike her.

"We're not going to be able to wait much longer, Dante," Todd proclaimed. "We can't afford to keep the production staff here if she's a no-show."

Dante nodded. "I know. It's just that her father has been ill." He reached into his pocket for his phone and called Adrianna, but it went straight to voice mail. Something was definitely wrong. "I can't reach her. I'm sorry, Todd, but we're going to have to cancel. I think it could be her father."

Todd nodded. "All right. Call me when you know something."

Dante barely heard him because he was already snatching off his microphone and heading to the door. He speed-dialed Adrianna from the elevator landing, but there was still no answer.

His car was waiting for him outside and Dante hopped inside. "We're going to the Hamptons and put a rush on it."

Dante was anxious during the ride. It didn't help that the clouds became dark and the skies opened, pouring down a sheet of rain, making the drive longer than Dante anticipated.

A sense of foreboding came over him when he arrived at the mansion and found the house surprisingly quiet. Usually staff was roaming the grounds, grooming the hedges or sweeping the front driveway, but now no one was in sight. He was more disturbed when he rang the doorbell and no one answered.

Dante tried the handle and found the door open. Quickly, he climbed the winding staircase to the second floor. He glanced down each hall, unsure of which one to take when he heard voices. He followed the sound until he came to a door cracked open.

The nurse and Nigel were sitting next to Adrianna's father. Dante cleared his throat and Nigel glanced up.

"Mr. Moore." Nigel wiped his eyes and Dante could tell he'd been crying. "I'm sorry. I didn't hear the door."

"It's all right, Nigel," Dante said, coming forward. "When Adrianna didn't answer her phone I was worried and just came over."

"Is that Dante?"

Dante heard a small whisper of a voice coming from the bed and couldn't imagine it was the once prominent man who'd threatened to destroy him if he didn't stay away from his daughter.

When Nigel moved out of the way, Dante was shocked by the sight of the man lying on the bed in front of him. This man was certainly not the Howard Wright he remembered. This man was emaciated. His face had sunk in and he appeared half the size he once was. "Mr. Wright?"

"So it is you," Howard Wright said once Dante made it to the bed.

Dante nodded. "It is. I'm sorry to see you like this."

"Are you really? I would think you would be happy to see me get what I had coming considering what I did to keep you away from my daughter."

"You're Adrianna's father," Dante responded. "I would never wish you ill."

"That's very kind of you," Howard said. "Nigel, I'd like to speak with Mr. Moore alone if you don't mind."

"No problem, Mr. Wright." The butler ushered the nurse out of the room.

"Don't tire him out," the nurse said to Dante before she left.

"I won't." Dante sat on the bed next to Adrianna's father. "What would you like to say to me, Mr. Wright?"

"Take care of my daughter," he murmured. "She's going to need you more than ever once I'm gone."

"That won't be a hardship. I love your daughter, Mr. Wright. I always have. And I promise I will take good care of Adrianna after you're gone." Truth be told, despite the relationships he'd had since Adrianna, he'd never truly loved anyone else. He'd found the love of his life when he was twenty-five and no one since had come close to ever taking her place.

"That's good because what I have to tell you now might change that, but I'm hoping that you can forgive her and forgive me."

Dante frowned. Whatever he had to say must be important because Mr. Wright was struggling to sit up, so Dante reached out, pulled him by the shoulders and propped him up against the pillows so he could sit up and face Dante eye to eye, man to man. "What do you have to tell me?"

"First off, my daughter has always loved you, but I refused to believe it. I thought I knew what was best for her."

"Father knows best?" Dante attempted a smile, trying to lighten the mood and make Mr. Wright feel better, but it wasn't working. Mr. Wright's expression was as stern as ever.

"I went to great lengths to keep you apart."

"How so?"

"Ten years ago, I lied to you, Dante. Adrianna didn't want to marry Phillip."

"She didn't?"

"No. I forced her to marry him."

"Why would do that?" Dante asked. "And more importantly, how could you force a grown woman to do something she didn't want to do?"

"Why? Because…" Howard starting coughing uncontrollably and Dante leaned over to the nightstand and poured him a glass of water. He placed the glass to Mr. Wright's lips and helped him drink the water.

After a short while, Howard spoke again. "Because I thought a lowly cook wasn't worthy of my daughter. I was governor of New York for Christ's sake. My daughter deserved to marry royalty, but fate turned against me. So I had to use some underhanded methods to get Adrianna to agree to do what I wanted."

Dante was horrified by what he was hearing. "What did you do? How did you get Adrianna to go along with your plan?"

"Well…" Howard lowered his head.

He was clearly ashamed of whatever he'd done, but the waiting was driving Dante mad. "Spit it out, Mr. Wright. You obviously want to clear your conscience before you leave this earth, so tell me what you did."

"Fate was on your side because imagine my surprise when my daughter turned up pregnant with your child."

"Excuse me!" Dante jumped off the bed. What was he talking about? Pregnant? Adrianna had never mentioned a child, not then and not now.

"When I realized that my twenty-year-old daughter

was unmarried and pregnant, I knew what I had to do," Howard responded. "I told her in no uncertain terms that either she marry the man I'd chosen for her or I'd cut her and her bastard child off and they'd be penniless and on the streets."

The enormity of Howard's words began to sink in, sending Dante back to the past and reminding him of how sudden Adrianna's marriage to Phillip had felt. Back then, he'd been stunned when Howard had told him that Adrianna was seeing another man, but he'd believed him because Adrianna had steadfastly refused to accept his calls or speak with him. He'd wanted to confront her about her betrayal and lies, but had never gotten the chance. If he had, perhaps he would have realized the truth.

Howard watched Dante's expression. "I'm sure you're remembering our conversation ten years ago, when I told you Adrianna didn't love you. It was a lie. She loved you a great deal, but she was concerned for the welfare of her child. I convinced her that the two of you and a newborn child would never survive on your salary. I took advantage of the fact that she was young and naive. She believed me and did as I asked."

"So you blackmailed your own daughter into marrying another man while she was carrying my child?" Dante was horrified by the man's actions. No wonder he wanted to clear his conscience before he died. "And now you want absolution for your sins?"

"No." Howard shook his head. "I don't deserve that. I just felt I owed you the truth. I was wrong back then. You are undoubtedly the right man for my daughter. She's lucky to have a man like you and I know that you're going to take care of my baby girl when I'm gone and she's all alone."

Dante ran his hands over his head, trying to absorb the humongous load the old man had just dropped on him. He walked over to the window and stared at the falling rain. That's when it hit him and he spun around. "And the baby?" Dante yelled. "What about the baby? What happened to my baby?"

"Father, don't!" Adrianna screamed from behind Dante.

Dante spun on his heel and came face-to-face with Adrianna who was trembling in the doorway.

"Please let me tell him," she cried. "He deserves to hear the rest from me."

Howard Wright nodded. He was exhausted from the effort and sank down into the bed.

Dante stared back at Adrianna, trying to find the woman he loved, but maybe didn't know at all. Not if she could keep something this huge from him. "Well, I'm waiting for an answer. What happened to my child?"

Tears trickled down Adrianna's cheeks as the moment she'd dreaded since Dante had burst into her office at *Foodies* magazine came to pass. "I lost the baby." Although it hurt, saying the words aloud felt like a giant weight had been lifted off her shoulders.

Dante nodded. "You lost our baby?"

"Yes. And I'm so sorry I didn't tell you, Dante." Her eyes were clouded with tears. "I wanted to so many times and then when you told me you loved me and vowed to leave the past in the past... I..."

"You thought you were off the hook. It allowed you to keep your dirty little secret in the dark."

"That's not true," Adrianna cried.

"No?" Dante laughed bitterly. "You were so afraid of

your father cutting off your inheritance that you agreed to marry a man you didn't love all in the name of money. My God, have you no shame, woman?"

"It wasn't like that, Dante," Adrianna murmured. "I admit I was young and stupid, but I did it for the right reasons. I did it for our child. To make sure he or she would have the best possible start in life."

"Unlike me, the poor orphan," Dante spat. "You chose money over me."

"I know it seems that way, but I didn't have a choice."

"Oh, you had a choice," Dante responded, pointing a finger at her. "You could have told me, but you didn't. You were prepared to live a lie. Had the child lived, you would have kept him or her from me. You would have denied me my child. To know that you would have never told me the truth, it's like you've plunged a knife into my heart and twisted it."

"Honestly, I don't know what I would have done had the baby lived. Maybe I would have changed my mind." Adrianna bunched her shoulders. "But what I can tell you is that losing our child after carrying it for five months was the hardest thing I've ever been through in my life outside of losing my mother and now my father." Adrianna pointed to her father in the bed.

"Well, here's what I know now." Dante headed toward the bedroom door. "You're a liar. Even after we've pledged our undying love for each other you still couldn't come clean with me." Dante reached for the door handle. "You're incapable of being honest."

"Please, Dante." Adrianna grabbed his arm. "Please don't leave like this. Please let me try to explain."

Dante snatched his hand away as if he'd been burned,

which he had—for a second time. "You already did. And what you did is unforgivable." And with those words, he walked out the door.

"Ohmigod!" Adrianna slumped to the floor in a heap. "I've lost him for good."

Chapter 12

"Wow!" Quentin was shocked when Dante summoned them to his condo later the following evening and revealed the secret Adrianna had been keeping for the past decade.

Dante had spent the previous evening alone, trying to process the shocking information he'd received and still couldn't make sense of it. He needed his family more than ever.

"That lying, deceitful witch." Sage couldn't believe her ears. "She kept the truth from you this entire time?" It was unfathomable that Adrianna would keep something so fundamental from Dante. She could only imagine what the news was doing to Dante.

"And would have kept on lying," Dante returned, plopping down on his leather couch, but he immediately sat up. "Even after I told her I loved her, she kept the truth from me. Had her father on his deathbed not had a conscience and felt the need to unload, I would have never known."

"I am so sorry, man." Malik was sympathetic as he sat in the armchair across from him. He knew how much Dante loved Adrianna and it broke his heart to see him in such pain.

"I knew she was hiding the fact that she was pregnant, but not this." As soon as the words slipped out of her mouth, Sage regretted saying them.

"Now is not the time to say I told you so," Quentin whispered harshly. It was the last thing Dante wanted to hear.

"What did you just say?" Dante asked, turning to glare at Sage.

Sage immediately lowered her head. "Nothing. I didn't say anything."

"You knew about this and didn't tell me?"

With Dante's eyes peering into hers beseechingly, Sage caved. "Okay, okay. I had my private investigator do a background check on her a few weeks back."

"You had Adrianna investigated?" Dante was floored by the lengths Sage would go in order to protect him.

"Well, I had good reason. Adrianna was so cagey. I knew something wasn't right." Sage defended herself. "My investigator found out she'd been pregnant when she was married, but Dante, I had no idea it was your child. I just assumed she'd been cheating with her ex-husband while with you. And when I found out she lost the baby, I just assumed she didn't want you to know and it wasn't my place to tell you. Trust me. I had no idea the depth of her lies."

Dante looked into Sage's heart and knew she was telling the truth. "It's okay." Dante held up his hand to Sage's protestations. "I believe you. I mean, wasn't I the one who told you to back off Adrianna? I doubt I would have listened if you'd tried to tell me the truth."

"It's what we told Sage," Quentin replied. "It wasn't her place or ours to tell you. It was Adrianna's."

"And she failed miserably," Dante replied. "And you know what hurts the most is that she knew how we grew up." He pointed to the three of them. "She knew I would never abandon my child, so she knowingly decided to keep my child from me. If she had her way, my child would have grown up never knowing I existed."

"What she did was wrong," Quentin responded, "but her father. To do that to his own child? What kind of man is he?" Even if he didn't approve of her choices, Quentin couldn't even imagine doing that to his baby girl, Bella.

"The worst kind," Malik said. "He may not have laid a hand on her, but it was emotional abuse. What he did was paramount to child abuse." Abuse was hot-button for Malik and he was sickened by what Adrianna's father had done. It was why he was in counseling, to make sure he was the best father he could be. He never wanted his past history of child abuse to ever come back and affect his unborn child.

"That doesn't make what she did right." Dante refused to make excuses for her behavior. "She was old enough to know better, Malik. And you know what makes this so hard to swallow?"

"What's that?" Quentin asked.

"That she duped me twice. I mean, c'mon. Fool me once, shame on you, but fool me *twice,* shame on me. I was a sucker and played right into her hands. It makes everything she's done since we reconnected suspect."

"Are you saying you don't believe she truly fell for

you again?" Sage asked, because even she would have to disagree. Despite her lies, Adrianna's feelings for Dante did appear genuine.

"What I believe is that she set this all in motion by giving me that good review. Guess she wanted a do-over and gullible Dante fell for her charms again."

"Don't do that." Sage fell to her knees and scooted next to Dante. "Your big and forgiving heart is what makes you you. It's what we love about you. Don't let Adrianna change that quality in you. It would be a travesty."

"I don't have much choice but to carry on," Dante replied. "We're joined at the hip until these twelve episodes of *Easy Entertaining* are over. And I for one can't wait for them to be done."

Adrianna had thought her father's last days were near after his confession to Dante, but the old man had a tough constitution because he was still with them. Todd sent a lovely basket to their home in the Hamptons and called to see if she could come in and finish taping the last two episodes of *Easy Entertaining* that week so they could start airing the show. She hadn't wanted to face Dante, but the show needed her and she didn't want it delayed because of her, so she made the drive into Manhattan.

Adrianna had no idea what the mood in the studio was going to be when she walked in on Friday. How would Dante treat her? She hadn't seen him since he'd stormed out her home a few days ago and despite her urgent pleas for him to call her, he'd remained silent.

When she arrived to the studio, Dante was already dressed in a pullover sweater and khaki pants and speaking with a member of the production team.

A member of the production crew said, "Hi, Adrianna. Welcome back."

"Thanks, I'm happy to be back." Dante had to have heard her, so she glanced in his direction for several long excruciating minutes, willing him to look at her, but he never did. It was as if he was refusing to acknowledge her presence.

Adrianna swallowed hard as she walked to the dressing area. She'd known it was going to be difficult, but this was downright painful. She gave the makeup artist a small, shy smile as she took a seat.

"How's your dad, Adrianna?" the makeup artist asked.

"He's hanging in there, Sheila. Thanks for asking."

"I give you props for coming in," Sheila replied. "Not so sure I could do the same."

"You'd be surprised," Adrianna responded. "Sometimes what you need is to get away for a breather."

Sheila nodded and began to work on Adrianna's face.

From across the room, Dante was doing his best to ignore the beautiful woman in the director's chair getting her hair and makeup done. He was livid with Adrianna for the huge secret she'd kept from him for over a decade that he could hardly see straight. She had denied him the right to be a father, hadn't even told him that she was pregnant, that they'd created a child together.

She'd used the fact that he'd wanted the past to remain in the past as an excuse not to tell him the truth. How could she keep something like that to herself after he'd told her he loved her? How could she look herself in the mirror knowing she was lying to him every day?

It showed him that he didn't really know Adrianna at all and clearly hadn't ten years ago, either. If so, she would never have kept such a secret to herself. Considering he'd been abandoned, he would never have done that to his own child. And Adrianna knew that. She knew how important being a father was to him.

Worst of all, he'd had to hear the truth from her father on his deathbed. If the old man hadn't spoken up, would she have ever told him they'd lost a child?

Dante was going to have to keep his distance as best he could until the last two episodes were taped because they very well might be his last.

Ian walked in about half an hour later and came toward Dante on the set of *Easy Entertaining*. "Dante, good to see you." He shook his hand.

"You as well," Dante replied. He'd just been reading through several of the cue cards to make sure he knew his mark and where to stand and when to face the camera.

"Well, I'm here to watch the last couple of episodes and see magic in the making," Ian returned. "The edits I have seen so far of the show have been great. So, I thought I'd check it out for myself firsthand."

Great, thought Dante, now he would have the boss looking over his shoulder. It was exactly what he didn't need today.

"All right, everyone," the production editor yelled out. "Places, please."

Slowly, Adrianna walked over from hair and makeup to join Dante on set. When she took a step closer to him to make sure she was in the frame, he moved away.

"Dante," the director said. "I need the two of you closer." He motioned for Dante to move closer to Adrianna.

"All right." Dante's mouth formed into a thin line and

Adrianna could sense he didn't want to be next to her. Anger was emanating from his every pore.

"Dante," she whispered, desperately trying to connect with him.

"Don't say a word," Dante hissed.

"We're taping in one, two, three…" The director threw down his hand.

"Today, we're going to be making herb-crusted pork tenderloin," Dante read from the cue cards as he looked into the camera dead-on.

"Along with a smooth creamy parmesan risotto," Adrianna added.

"Let's get started by gathering our ingredients." Dante swiftly moved away from Adrianna and headed for the fridge and began piling his arms with an assortment of fresh herbs and spices.

"While Dante is chopping the herbs," Adrianna said, "I'm going to heat a saucepan with water to start my risotto."

Dante was continuing with the pork when he heard, "Stop!"

"Is it me or are our hosts extremely tense?" Ian asked, turning to Todd at his side from the control room. "And lacking chemistry. What happened? The last time I was here they oozed it."

"It's not just you," Todd replied and stepped onto set. "Okay, you two." He pulled Dante and Adrianna aside. "We're not getting your usual enthusiasm and fire on screen. Adrianna, was this too soon for you to come back to work?"

"No." Adrianna shook her head. She was trying her best to put up a good front. Guess she wasn't doing a good job of it. "I needed the distraction."

"All right." Todd eyed her carefully, trying to determine if he could believe her, but she appeared to be telling the truth. "Okay. Let's try another take." Todd motioned for the director to cue taping again and stepped to the side.

"Get it together, Adrianna," Dante hissed from underneath his breath. "I won't let you blow this."

"It's not my fault you won't talk to me." Adrianna turned suddenly to face Dante.

As soon as the cameras began rolling, Dante tried turning on the charm, while Adrianna struggled to feign a smile. Dante had just begun marinating the pork with a mixture of olive oil and spices when Todd yelled, "Cut!"

Dante and Adrianne looked up. "This isn't working," Todd said. "Let's take a ten-minute break and reconvene."

"Fine." Dante stalked off set.

"Is there a problem?" Todd asked Adrianna.

"No." She lowered her head and quickly rushed off to the ladies' room.

When she returned five minutes later to set after a touch-up of her makeup, Dante was already on set. She hoped he was more amenable and they could pull off these last two episodes with some modicum of decorum, but it wasn't to be so.

When she made a mistake in the order of starting their dish together, Dante snapped at her. "What the hell are you doing?"

"There's no need for you to yell at me, Dante," Adrianna returned. "It was a mistake. I realize you're upset with me, but if you just gave me a chance—"

"To what, explain?" Dante laughed derisively. "You can't explain. It's your fault we're in this mess. Thanks to you and your lies."

This time it was Ian that came rushing out of the control room yelling. "Stop!" He stormed toward the duo. "I don't know what is going on between the two of you and I really don't need to know. But you are wasting *my* and everyone else's time and I don't appreciate it. Behave like professionals or else this show will never see the light of day." Ian stared back and forth between the duo. "Have I made myself clear?"

"Crystal," Dante stated. He wasn't about to let Adrianna ruin this for him. He'd worked too hard and long to get himself in this position and he wasn't about to blow it. He would suck up his anger toward her and put on the best show possible.

"Then let's begin again." Ian motioned to the director to start up.

Taking a deep breath, Adrianna willed her nerves to calm down and faced the camera. The rest of episode continued with their usual smiles, cooking tips and a few familial anecdotes. Afterward, Dante was glad it was over and he could remove the plastic smile he'd plastered on his face for the duration of the two episodes.

"Good job," Ian said to Dante once they'd finished taping and he was walking off set. "I'm sorry I had to be harsh before. I just had to snap you both out of whatever was going on between you. I needed you to make magic."

"You were right," Dante responded as he removed the makeup from his face. He'd gotten used to doing it himself. "We're professionals and we should behave as such."

"Well, I know how hard it can be when you're working with someone you're in a relationship with." He and Sage had gone through something similar when they'd been dating secretly.

"You needn't worry about that anymore," Dante replied, "because Adrianna and are I over."

"You are?" Ian was stunned. Sage hadn't mentioned anything to him.

Dante nodded. He'd asked Sage to keep his personal business private and apparently she had.

"Well, I guess that explains the hostility that you were giving off at the start of the taping." Ian rubbed his chin thoughtfully. "I'm truly sorry to hear it, but you do realize that I have a lot of press planned for you and Adrianna over the next week to promote the show. Are you going to be able to handle that?"

"Absolutely," Dante replied. "As you said, we are professionals." He'd pushed down his feelings for Adrianna before and he would do so again. He would do whatever was necessary to ensure the show would go on.

"This really wasn't necessary, Madison," Adrianna said as her cousin pulled her inside the local health club in the Hamptons for a yoga class on Saturday morning. Madison had barely given her time to throw on her yoga pants, sports bra and tank top before she'd hustled Adrianna out of the house.

Her cousin was already attired in her snazzy matching gym outfit complete with makeup and perfume. Were they going to the gym to work out or to be seen by the local muscle men?

"It's exactly what you need to decompress," Madison responded. "You've been worried sick about Uncle Howard and to top it all off you and Dante have hit a snag."

Adrianna sighed. "It's more than a snag, Madison.

Dante is through with me." She stuffed her gym bag into a locker in the women's locker room.

"Why, did something else happen?" Madison asked as she completed a quick series of stretches before class. Adrianna had called her several days ago weeping that Uncle Howard had told Dante the truth about why she'd married Phillip. Poor thing had been devastated.

"Do you mean when he barely looked at me while we taped the television show or his steadfast refusal to return a single one of my phone calls?" she asked, grabbing her mat and heading for the doorway.

"All of the above," Madison offered and opened the door to the yoga class for Adrianna to enter.

"He's so upset with me, Madison," Adrianna said as she placed her mat on the floor. "I know I could get through to him if he just gave me a chance. I don't want to lose him again."

"Let's talk more after class. You need this more than ever," Madison said, joining her on the floor.

Adrianna sat cross-legged with her hands on her knees and tried to focus on her breathing. She kept her spine straight as the teacher suggested and pushed her backside down into the floor. She raised her hands over her head and slowly exhaled, bringing down her arms each time. She repeated it several times until she began to relax.

They moved to the dog and cat positions. She was on all fours with her legs and hips apart, tilted her pelvis up and then down. Then it was on to the mountain position in which she was on her toes to the forward extension bend. It felt good because it stretched her legs and back.

When the hour-long yoga session was over, Adrianna felt her balance and concentration was much improved.

"See, didn't that make you feel better?" Madison asked when they went back to the locker room to collect their belongings.

"Much, thanks." Adrianna patted the perspiration on her brow with her towel and took a sip of water from her bottle. "I'm surprised how much of a workout yoga really is."

"How about a smoothie?" Madison asked once she'd grabbed her gym bag out of the locker.

"Hmm…" Adrianna moaned. "Sounds perfect."

The smoothie store was in the perfect location, right next door to the gym. Adrianna ordered a strawberry and peach smoothie with an energy booster. It was exactly what she would need to get her through the long night with her father. Sometimes she sent the nurse home and sat with her father during the night, tending to his needs. They would reminisce about when he was running for office or the elation he felt when he won an election. It was in those moments that Adrianna would see a spark of her father's former self.

"Can I ask you something?" Madison asked, taking a seat on the barstool while she waited for her smoothie to be prepared.

"What's that?"

"Do you think Uncle Howard told Dante on purpose to sabotage your relationship?"

Adrianna paused and reflected on Madison's question. "I've wondered that myself, but when I asked him about it he denied it. He said he just wanted to clear his conscience. He was surprised to find out that I hadn't told Dante. I mean, how can I blame him? I had tons of opportunities to tell Dante myself and I didn't."

"I guess I didn't offer you the best advice," Madison

responded. She accepted her smoothie from the cashier and handed her a five. "Keep the change."

"Don't go blaming yourself, either." Adrianna pointed her finger at Madison. "The blame rests entirely upon my shoulders. It's just that I love Dante and I want him back and I'm hoping that maybe not now, but one day, he'll forgive me."

Chapter 13

"Ladies and gentlemen, we are so excited to have the hosts of *Easy Entertaining,* Dante Moore and Adrianna Wright, with us this afternoon," Angie Taylor, radio host for Hot 97 FM said on Monday.

Lawrence Enterprises had arranged a press tour for them and Dante and Adrianna had a full slate of guest appearances on radio and television during the week as well as a print interview with *CRAZE*.

They'd arrived about fifteen minutes prior to allow the production crew to give them headsets and add extra microphones to the interview table.

"Thank you, Angie," Dante said. "We're excited to be here to promote the show."

"How did you both get into cooking?" Angie asked. "We'll start with you, Adrianna."

"Well, I grew up with a cook that always prepared my meals for me, but I still loved to go into the kitchen and try the new dishes the cook was preparing for our family. Eventually, when I graduated high school, I decided to pursue the culinary arts."

"Your bio reads that you studied in Paris at Le Cordon Bleu," Angie continued. "That's quite an accomplishment."

"Yes, I did. It was an amazing experience getting to work with chefs of that caliber."

"And you, Dante. You're the owner of two fantastic restaurants right here in Manhattan. Tell us about them."

"Yes, I own Dante's tapas bar in Greenwich Village. It's been open for about five years and Renaissance, my new restaurant, specializing in New American cuisine with a soul food twist, opened in Harlem about six months ago," Dante replied. "They each offer me a chance to explore a different culinary point of view."

"And what point of view will you be trying to get across to viewers of *Easy Entertaining?*"

"That cooking can be fun," Adrianna replied.

"It doesn't have to be hard," Dante added. "With a little planning and some fresh ingredients, you can make some great dishes to entertain either your family or a large group."

"Well, I thank you both for stopping by Hot 97," Angie replied, speaking into the mike. "And you can catch the debut of *Easy Entertaining* on Sunday at 10:00 a.m. on WTTG.

"Thanks, guys," Angie said as Dante took his microphone off his lapel. "You gave my listeners exactly the tidbits they needed to hear."

"Thanks for having us." Dante shook her hand.

"And I look forward to having you on the show again," Angie responded. "Best of luck."

* * *

Two days later, it was off to a morning news show. Dante and Adrianna climbed into the limousine waiting for them at the curb. Ian had hired the limo to drive them around while on company business. Still the gentleman, Dante held open the door for Adrianna and with as much decorum as she could in her pencil-straight black skirt and button-down cardigan, she slid inside. She noticed Dante's eyes roving her bare legs just as he closed the door behind her. Had she imagined it? Or was it just a wish fulfillment?

Dante had been keeping his distance. First it was the radio show, then the interview with *CRAZE* and yesterday a photograph and review in the *New York Post*. It was driving Adrianna mad even more so because he was silent during the ride to the news program.

The air inside the vehicle was thick with anger and regret. Dante was still furious with her for keeping the truth that she'd been pregnant with his child and Adrianna because she had failed to tell him the truth herself.

She'd had countless sleepless nights over the past couple of weeks. She'd lain awake in bed and dreamed of the passion they'd shared together and what might never be again. And she had only herself to blame. Dante had forgiven her for marrying another man and would have forgiven her this, too, if only she'd told him sooner.

"We're almost there," the driver said.

Dante pressed the intercom. "Great, thanks." He lowered his head and continued flipping through the magazine he'd been reading.

"Are you ever going to speak to me again?" Adrianna asked, swiveling around to face him. "Or are you just going to sit there and ignore me all day?"

"The latter," Dante responded, not looking up. Did

she think it was easy for him to ignore her after all they'd shared? It wasn't, but he refused to be lied to. He deserved better from the woman who said she loved him. He deserved a woman who was open and honest with him. And Adrianna wasn't that woman.

"As you wish." Adrianna turned around and faced the window. Taking a deep breath, she willed herself not to cry. She refused to mess up perfectly good makeup. If he wanted to behave as if they'd never meant anything to each other, then she would try and do the same.

As if he was Dr. Jekyll/Mr. Hyde, Dante changed into a completely different man in front of the camera at the news station. Adrianna was amazed at how he could turn his emotions on and off. In the green room while they'd waited for their segment, he'd been cold and unfeeling. In front of the cameras, he was warm and kind to her, even a little bit flirtatious.

"How long have the two of you been working together?" the newscaster asked.

"Only a few months," Dante answered quickly.

"Well, you could have fooled me." She laughed. "It seems like you've been a team for years."

"Thank you." Adrianna's mouth creased into a smile.

"So what are you making for us today?" the host inquired.

"We're going to be teasing you and the viewers' tummies with some flank steak with chimicurri on crostinis," Dante said.

"Sounds delicious." The host grinned. "And while these chefs prep, we're going to go to commercial break."

"And cut!" the director yelled.

"You two are doing fantastic," the newscaster said. "You're naturals."

The ten-minute segment went smoothly as if it had been prerecorded. Adrianna prepared the ingredients for the chimicurri, the cilantro, parsley, mint and garlic, during the break. When they returned, she added the olive oil, red vinegar and a little salt and pepper to the mixture.

"Taste that." Adrianna gave the host a little spoonful of the chimicurri sauce.

"That is *sooo*...good and flavorful."

"That's what *Easy Entertaining* is all about," Dante chimed in as he grilled the flank steak he'd already pre-marinated in red wine, garlic and salt and pepper.

Once the steak was done, he sliced it across the grain. After a brush of oil, he added the sliced baguette on the grill, let it crisp and then topped it with the steak and chimicurri sauce.

"How about we have a taste?" Dante asked the host.

"You're going to love this," Adrianna added. "All the flavors combine to make one great bite."

They each grabbed a piece of crostini and took a nibble.

"Everyone, that was divine. You're going to love this recipe," the host gushed into the camera. "And I'm sure a whole lot more on *Easy Entertaining* premiering Sunday at ten o'clock on WTTG."

"Good job." Dante gave Adrianna a fist bump when the taping was over. It was the first friendly gesture Dante had made toward Adrianna in weeks. She was happy for just some sign that he didn't despise her.

"You, too." Adrianna smiled.

"Saw you on the morning show," Sage said, joining Dante in the Renaissance kitchen that evening.

"Yeah, how was I?" Dante inquired, looking up from the homemade gnocchi he was making.

"You were quite good considering you were standing next to the woman who betrayed you."

Dante laughed derisively. "Yeah, there's that." He moved from the counter to stir the white truffle sauce on a slow simmer on the stove.

"But who you're still obviously head over heels for," Sage commented, tilting her head so she could glance at Dante, who was doing his best to avoid her gaze by furiously stirring the sauce.

"Sage, don't start."

"Start what?"

Dante glanced in her direction. "Meddling, what you do best."

"Do I meddle?" Sage said it as a rhetorical question even though she already knew the answer. She did have a tendency to stick her nose where it didn't belong. "Okay, yes, I do meddle. But even I can see how besotted you are with the woman."

"And that means absolutely nothing without trust. I don't trust her, Sage, and doubt I ever could again. If she could lie to me about carrying my child, what else would she keep from me? How could I trust her with my heart?"

Sage paused. She didn't have a quick response for that question. "True, I don't deny trust is important. I guess that's why I've kept Ian at bay for nearly a year. He wants to marry me, but it's been hard for me to make that final step. I'm afraid because of his playboy reputation and because I don't want to get hurt. But I don't want that for you, Dante. Despite how you feel about Adrianna, I want you to be happy even if it is with her."

"I thought you didn't like Adrianna."

Sage smiled. "I don't, but if she's the person that does it for you, then who am I stand in your way?"

Dante shook his head. "You are not standing in my way, Sage. Your silence allowed Adrianna to dig her own grave. She broke us, not you."

"But I…"

"Sage, I appreciate you trying, but not even you can wave a magic wand and make what Adrianna did suddenly okay."

"There's nothing I can do?" She was crestfallen. "I'm used to fixing things." As an attorney, it was her specialty to come up with a solution.

"I know, kiddo," Dante put down the knife he was using, wiped his hand on his apron and came over to stroke her cheek. "But some things, once broken, can't be fixed. Work on you," he suggested. "And finally allow Ian to put a ring on it."

Sage threw back her head and laughed. "Since when did you start quoting Beyoncé?"

"When my hardheaded little sister keeps playing hard to get." He pinched her nose.

Sage slapped his hand away. "I hated when Q did it and I don't like you doing it now."

"Stop being a little brat then and go home to your man." He pushed her toward the door.

"And what about you?" Sage asked from the double doors that opened to the dining room. "I don't want to leave you alone."

"Don't worry about me," Dante responded, going back to the stove. "I'm used to it."

Sage didn't like his comment, but knew when to leave well enough alone and walked out the door. It was then that Dante allowed himself to feel the hurt and anger bottled up inside. He reached for a bottle of white wine on the counter and flung it across the room. It shattered into tiny little pieces just like his heart.

"You and Adrianna have exceeded my expectations," Ian told Dante and Adrianna on Friday evening after their short press tour was over. "The buzz we've been getting is fantastic."

Ian had graciously invited them to share a drink at his penthouse in Central Park West. Dante hadn't wanted to attend, but figured he owed Ian for giving him the chance to show what he was made of.

They were now sitting on his Italian leather sofa making small talk. Sitting next to Adrianna was the last place in the world Dante wanted to be. For days, he'd had to endure a mixture of emotions from anger and wanting to ream Adrianna out to desire flowing hot and heavy through his veins to a lower part of his anatomy. The same pull he'd always felt for her was right underneath the surface, and try as he might, he was having a hard time letting go.

Adrianna felt a deep physical yearning in her lower belly. She fought to ignore it, but even from where she sat, she could still smell his robust, manly scent.

"I think you two have what it takes to go the distance," Ian said, offering them both a flute of champagne to toast.

"What's this for?" Adrianna accepted the champagne.

"For the great job you've done and for the next step in your television future," Ian stated.

"What do you mean?" Dante asked. His eyes darkened with emotion. "We've fulfilled our obligation to tape twelve episodes."

"True." Ian rubbed his jaw. "But I was thinking of something more permanent."

"Are you serious?" Adrianna's mouth dropped open.

"Absolutely." Ian laughed at her surprised expression. "I'm convinced that you have what it takes to make *Easy Entertaining* a success and coincidentally make you both household names, which is why I want you to continue the show. How does that sound?"

"That sounds fabulous!" Adrianna was thrilled.

Dante remained quiet.

"Is there a problem?" Ian asked, noting the stern look on Dante's face. "I thought you would be excited by this news. This is what you wanted, yes?"

"It is, but at what cost?" Dante wrung his hands in his lap.

"I don't understand." Ian was perplexed by Dante's less than enthusiastic response.

"It's simple," Dante replied sharply. "I never wanted this arrangement to begin with and now that I've fulfilled my obligation, there's no point in continuing."

"Dante, please…" Tears welled in Adrianna's eyes as she saw her dream slipping away. "Please don't do this."

Dante ignored her pleas. "Doing this show was a great learning experience, Ian, and it has shown me that I have the chops to do this. And with a little time and patience, I can have my *own* show."

"I see." Ian's vexation was evident by the bridled anger in his voice. "You do realize that there's a clause in your contract which expresses that LE has the right to pick up an option on the show."

"You're welcome to try and exercise it," Dante returned. His voice was firm and final. "But I think you've seen what it's like when Adrianna and I don't connect. It's utter chaos. Imagine if you force us into the arrangement. for an entire season." Dante rose from the sofa without touching his champagne and placed the glass on the cocktail table. "And before you even mention money, don't bother because in case you didn't know, Ian, money can't buy everything. Excuse me." Dante marched past them and out the door.

"Wow! I knew you two had a disagreement," Ian replied, "but after the last week promoting the show I thought you'd gotten past it."

Adrianna shook her head and reached for her purse to grab a tissue. "I knew better," she murmured. "And now watching him walk out the door, I know that it's truly over between us."

Chapter 14

Adrianna thought she'd reached her limit when Dante had walked out of Ian's penthouse and never looked back. She'd thought that was the worst life had in store that day. She was wrong.

When she pulled into the driveway and saw Dr. Baker's car, she knew it was time.

Her father had struggled to stay alive for as long as he could but the end was here. The realization shot an aching pain straight to Adrianna's heart and her anguish peaked to shatter the last shreds of her control. Before she knew what she was doing, she was beating the steering wheel in frustration.

After she'd let it all out, Adrianna knew what she needed to do. Taking a ragged breath, Adrianna took a long, deep breath and then went inside the mansion to say good-bye to her father.

Nigel was outside the bedroom door sitting on a bench.

Too caught up in his own grief, he jumped when he heard her approach.

"It's going to be all right, Nigel," Adrianna found the inner strength to touch his shoulder and say. "We'll get through this."

Nigel was so overcome he couldn't speak, so Adrianna went inside without him. She found Dr. Baker and the nurse at her father's bedside.

"Adrianna, I'm so glad you're here," Dr. Baker said, reaching for her hand. "I'm not sure how much longer he could have held on."

"Thank you, Dr. Baker, for being here." She squeezed his hand.

"It's time, Adrianna," Dr. Baker whispered in her ear, "to say your good-byes."

Adrianna nodded and kneeled down by her father's bedside.

"I love you, baby girl," her father managed to eke out. "I know I may not have always been the best father, but one thing has never altered and that's my love for you. You are and will always be the light of my life."

A lone tear slid down Adrianna's cheek. "I love you, too, Daddy," she whispered, grasping his frail hand in hers. "And you can leave this earth knowing that I forgive you, Daddy. Okay? I forgive you."

Seconds later, his eyes closed and Adrianna dropped her head to his chest and sobbed.

Dante was deep into cooking for a catering event when Malik stopped by. He'd accepted a last-minute wedding for one hundred fifty people just to keep his mind off Adrianna and his career. The only way he knew how to not think about her was work. Hard, demanding work.

He was roasting several racks of lamb, making trays

of homemade scalloped potatoes and grilling bunches of asparagus for the wedding. He'd been prepping in Renaissance's kitchen for the past forty-eight hours and had tuned out the world. It was a daunting task, but it would keep his mind off what he might never have. Quentin, Malik and Sage had called him several times, but he'd ignored them. He knew they wanted to talk to him about the end of his relationship with Adrianna or perhaps his turning down Ian's offer to continue the show. Either way, he hadn't wanted any advice or suggestions on his love life or career or lack thereof.

"Hey, man, what are you doing here?" Dante asked when Malik popped his head in and saw the kitchen in utter chaos. "Shouldn't you be at Peyton's side? Isn't she due to deliver any minute?"

"No and yes," Malik replied. "My purpose here is dual fold. First, you forgot our standing gym date."

It was then that Dante glanced up from wrapping up the scalloped potatoes to see Malik wearing jogging pants and a T-shirt.

"I'm sorry, Malik. I got completely caught up in preparing for this wedding," Dante responded. "My apologies."

"I figured as much," Malik said, walking toward him. "It's not like you to stand me up which is why I came. Sage told me that you turned down Ian's offer to continue *Easy Entertaining* after the twelve episodes air. Are you sure that's the way you want to go?"

"Turning it down wasn't easy," Dante said. "None of this is, Malik. I'm just having a hard time reconciling the woman I thought I knew back then with the woman I know today."

"I understand you're upset with Adrianna, but I have a feeling she's going to need you now more than ever."

"What do you mean?" Dante immediately stopped what he was doing and wiped his hands on his apron.

"You mean you haven't heard?"

Dante frowned. "Heard what?"

Malik pulled out a copy of the *New York Times* from his jogging pants pocket. "Adrianna's father, Howard Wright, died two days ago."

"Whoa!" Dante covered his mouth with his hand. "I knew it was coming, but it just seemed like the old man had a steel will. Even after his deathbed confession to me, he'd been holding on for weeks. Why didn't anyone bother to call me?"

"We tried and you didn't return any of our calls," Malik responded. "Sage assumed that your non-response meant that you didn't want to have anything more to do with her, but when you didn't show up at the gym, I realized I had better take matters into my own hands. I just couldn't picture you being this cold and unfeeling."

"Christ!" Dante rubbed his head. "Adrianna must be devastated. She may not have been close to her father, but she'd tried to make that up by moving back to New York. Do you know when the funeral is?"

Malik glanced down at the paper. "Day after tomorrow. Are you going to go?"

Dante didn't hesitate before answering. "Of course."

Malik smiled. Now *there* was the Dante he remembered.

"Have you heard from Dante?" Madison asked Adrianna as she helped her select a black suit to wear to her father's funeral that day. Adrianna had tried on half a dozen already until she'd found one that was acceptable.

Adrianna shook her head. "Not in person, but I

did receive flowers." And it had hurt. Flowers? How impersonal! She knew he hated her for what she'd done, but to not even call to pay his respects? It made the loss of her father all the more unbearable.

All the arrangements had been made for the funeral as her father's will was quite clear on the type of service he wished to have. It made Adrianna's life very simple. *Follow instructions. Put one foot in front the other. Don't think about all you've lost.*

"I just can't believe that Dante would behave this way." Madison was stunned. "He never struck me as the type to hold a grudge. He was always so kind and caring."

"I guess that's what happens when the woman you love breaks your heart twice. It turns it into a block of ice," Adrianna said coldly, twisting her hair into an unsophisticated bun. She didn't care how she looked. She just wanted to make it through the day without falling to pieces.

"Well, don't you worry," Madison replied. "If Mr. Dante Moore can't bother to be here, you've got me, kid. You remember that. You always got me."

"Thank you, Maddie," Adrianna cried, and gave her a hug.

Dante tightened the tie on his charcoal suit and glanced in the mirror. How had he gotten here? How could he be going to Adrianna's father's funeral and yet feel so far removed from the woman herself?

He hadn't called Adrianna because he hadn't known what to say. The usual platitudes of "I'm sorry for your loss" just didn't seem to cut it after all they'd shared. He felt helpless and unsure of what to do.

He was berating himself when the doorbell rang. When he opened it, Quentin, Malik and Sage were on the other side. They were all dressed in black suits and Sage was wearing a big black hat.

"You guys didn't have to do this," Dante began, but Sage silenced him with a finger to his lips.

"Don't you even go there," Sage replied. "This is what families do. We stand by each other's side."

"That's right," Quentin replied. "We're here to drive you to the funeral and service."

"We didn't want you to be alone," Malik added.

Dante nodded. "From the moment I met you guys, I have never been alone. And I thank God for it."

"And you never will be," Sage returned. The foursome crowded into a group bear hug.

They arrived at the church just before the service began. Dante chose to sit in the back podium as to not intrude on Adrianna and her family. He wasn't sure she would even want to see him as he'd been less than kind to her the last few times they'd seen each other.

It was an elaborate service with members of the House and Senate speaking on the former governor's behalf as well as a beautiful spiritual montage by a member of his church. Adrianna got particularly choked up when their butler, Nigel, went to the podium and spoke such kind words about her old man. She was keeping it together pretty well until she decided to speak the eulogy for her father.

"As the last member of my father's immediate family," Adrianna began, "I only felt it proper to speak on his behalf. My father, Howard Wright, was a proud family man. He was dedicated to serving the community and the great state of New York, but he loved his family even more. He loved his wife, my mother, Vanessa, deeply and only wanted the best for me, his only daughter. He wasn't without his faults because the old man knew how to push my buttons." Adrianna attempted to laugh, but instead it caught in her throat and she began to cough uncontrollably.

From the back of the room, Dante watched Adrianna struggle with her speech. He knew how important it was for her to speak, but he wasn't sure she could handle the grief of standing in front of a roomful of people, many of whom were strangers, and speak about her father in the third person.

Somehow she managed to continue to her speech. "But what I never doubted was his unwavering love for me."

Tears began to stream down Adrianna's face in earnest and it was then that Dante knew what he had to do. He rose and walked up the aisle toward her. He couldn't let her stand up there alone. Despite everything they'd been through, he'd promised her that she wouldn't go through her grief alone—at least not now.

"What are you doing?" Sage had whispered from his side as he left his seat, but Quentin quieted her.

"Let the man do what he's got to do," Quentin had said.

"He's got to protect his woman," Malik had replied. He knew the feeling. When Peyton had been hurt after an abused student assaulted her a year back, Malik had seen stars, so he could only imagine the thoughts running through Dante's mind as he saw the woman he loved in pain.

Adrianna tried to stop herself from crying and continue the beautiful speech she'd spent the past two days writing, but the grief just seemed to overtake her and a sob escaped her lips. It was then as she wiped her eyes with her father's handkerchief that she noticed a lone figure walking toward the podium. As the person got closer, through the mist of her tears, Adrianna recognized it was Dante.

What is he doing here? Why has he come?

Those weren't the questions she was thinking of; instead she was relieved, relieved to see the man she loved coming to rescue her from public embarrassment.

Without a word, Dante walked to the podium, wrapped his arms around Adrianna and led her off the stage. The minister took that as a sign that she was done and to continue with the service.

Dante led Adrianna to the first pew where Madison and her mother, Mimi, sat. They made room so Dante could sit beside her. And that's what he did. He sat next to Adrianna and held her hand for the duration of the service.

"I thought you weren't going to come," Adrianna spoke in a weak and tremulous whisper.

"Of course I'd be here. Where else would I be?"

Dante's voice had an infinitely compassionate tone. Adrianna glanced up and looked into Dante's warm brown eyes and found comfort in his inherent strength. He didn't have to come to the funeral. He owed Adrianna absolutely nothing, yet he'd come to hold her hand during one of the most devastating moments in her life. "Thank you." She squeezed his hand in recognition.

"You're welcome."

When it was time to walk down the aisle in the funeral procession, Dante was right by Adrianna's side. She leaned against him for support as she glanced around and saw all the sympathetic faces staring back at her. She was Howard and Vanessa Wright's only heir and would inherit a fortune, so the world was watching her, but Adrianna didn't care about the money. Because she would give anything to have her mother and father back with her.

When the limo pulled up to the curb for the family, Dante didn't hesitate for a moment to jump inside with Adrianna.

"We're so glad you're here, Mr. Moore," her Aunt Mimi said once the door had closed behind him. "Adrianna needed you."

"Glad I could be here," Dante said.

"It was a beautiful service," Madison commented, offering a weak smile to Adrianna.

Adrianna nodded and blankly stared out the window.

Later, she wouldn't remember much about the day. How sunny the sky was as they laid her father into the ground, or how white the gloves were that her father's pallbearers had given her or how good the food tasted at the repast. She would just remember that Dante had come through for her.

Once back at the mansion in the Hamptons, family, friends, colleagues and onlookers came to pay their respects to Adrianna. She stood there and accepted their condolences gracefully, but Dante could see she was torn up inside. He didn't know what to do except stand there. Nothing he could say would take away the pain she was feeling.

Quentin, Malik and Sage were some of the first to offer their condolences.

"We're so sorry for your loss." Quentin spoke first and leaned forward to give Adrianna a hug and kiss on the cheek.

"Thank you," Adrianna murmured, "for…for coming." Dante squeezed her hand.

"I know I'm the last person you might want to accept

help from," Sage spoke next, "but if you need anything—either of you—" she glanced in Dante's direction "—we are a phone call away."

"That's right," Malik added from behind her. "You're not alone." Malik patted Dante on the shoulder before the trio dispersed among the crowd.

Dante didn't know how long he and Adrianna stood there, shaking hands, receiving hugs and accepting condolences. When it was over, he was exhausted, so he could only imagine how emotionally drained Adrianna was. Once the crowd had finally begun to taper off, Dante decided to take Adrianna upstairs.

"I'm going to put her to bed," Dante told Madison.

"I think that's a good idea," Madison said. "The poor thing must be exhausted. I'll bring up a plate, too, in case she should get hungry."

"Thanks, Maddie." Dante patted her shoulder.

Instead of trying to walk Adrianna up, Dante lifted her limp body in his arms and carried her up the stairs. Dante found her room easily as it was covered with several different black dresses and suits. Dante shifted Adrianna in his arms and pushed the clothes off the bed. They landed in a heap on the floor.

Gently, Dante laid her down on the bed and Adrianna curled up in a ball. Dante reached down to the edge of the bed and pulled up a blanket to cover her trembling body. He was about to leave, so she could sleep, when Adrianna's hand peeked out from underneath the duvet and he heard her shaken voice. "Please don't go."

Those were the only words Dante needed to hear. He kicked off his loafers, removed his suit jacket and slid underneath the covers with her. He curled up behind Adrianna and spooned her in his arms until she fell asleep.

* * *

Dante awoke to the sun streaming into the windows and Adrianna in his arms directly facing him. Her legs were intertwined with his and her arms were wrapped around his midsection. Dante pushed a wayward curl out of her face and stared down at her. Losing a parent had to be difficult, but losing both had to be unbearable. He'd learned long ago to live without them because he'd never known his parents. He could sympathize with Adrianna's plight.

Adrianna's eyes popped open and the realization of what had happened must have hit her because she began to shake uncontrollably.

"It's okay, Adrianna," Dante whispered. His gut wrenched seeing her in so much agony. He wished he could take away some of the pain, but he couldn't. She had to feel it. "You will make it through this."

"I don't know…if I c-can." Adrianna hiccupped.

"In time you will mend and the pain will become less. It may not seem like that now, but it will."

"Will you be by my side?" Adrianna asked, looking up at him with tear-filled eyes.

"Yes, I will."

In the days that followed, along with her father's attorney, Dante helped Adrianna put her father's affairs in order. Adrianna wasn't sure what she would do with such a large house on her own, but she couldn't bear to part with her family home. The attorney agreed it wasn't smart for her to make rash decisions and promised to follow up with her in a few months.

Dante never left her side which was why Malik drove to his condo to pack some of Dante's clothes and bring them to the Hamptons.

"How is she holding up?" Malik asked when he arrived with a large suitcase in hand earlier in the week.

Dante shrugged. "As well as can be expected. How are Renaissance and Dante's?"

"Q and I checked in and your sous-chefs have everything under control until you return."

"Thank you. I truly appreciate it."

"We told you, we'd do anything we could for you."

"I know," Dante said, "but this is above and beyond the call of duty."

Malik frowned. "Like hell it is. You're family."

A grin overtook Dante's features. "I'm really lucky to have you guys. Adrianna's feeling pretty alone. I mean, she has her aunt Mimi and cousin Madison, but…"

"But it's not the same," Malik finished.

"You feel me."

"So how long will you be up here, you think?" Malik inquired.

"For a few days. I can't afford to stay too long, but I will until I think she's okay to be on her own."

"You're a good man, brother." Malik shook his hand on the way out.

"Give my love to Peyton," Dante said. "And let me know if I become an uncle while I'm out here."

"Now you know you will be one of the first to know." Malik laughed and gave him a hug. "Our prayers are with you."

"Was that Malik I heard?" Adrianna asked from the top of the stairs once the door had closed.

"Yes," Dante replied. "He brought me some supplies." Dante held up his suitcase.

Dante was staying for a while? Adrianna's heart leaped into her chest. It was the first time she felt she could smile since her father had passed. "That's great!" She tried not to sound too hopeful.

"How about some lunch, you two?" Nigel asked from the doorway to the kitchen. Adrianna hadn't eaten a bite since the day before and had to be famished.

"Nigel, you don't have to keep serving me," Adrianna said, coming down the stairs. "Father's gone."

Nigel hung his head low. "I know, but allow me to do this for you, Ms. Adrianna. At least for now."

"All right," Adrianna conceded. "But only if you sit down and eat with us. Shake on it?"

"Deal." Nigel shook her hand.

Adrianna plopped down on her bed in the dark several days later. She was completely drained. For the majority of the day, she, Dante and Nigel had packed most of her father's personal effects to deliver to charity. She hadn't wanted to do it so soon, but her father had been adamant that he hadn't wanted her holding on like he'd done when her mother had died.

Back then, her father had refused to allow anyone, including Adrianna, to remove anything that belonged to her mother from the house. It was as if he was keeping the room as a shrine to her. So, when he'd known the end was near for him, he'd made Adrianna promise not to do the same thing. She could keep a few things, but his will was clear that everything should be donated.

Dante turned on the lamp on the nightstand. "Are you okay?" he asked, sitting on her bed after taking off his sneakers. They'd managed to pack up over a dozen bags of clothing, shoes, books and the like.

Adrianna nodded. "Yeah, I'm just tired."

Dante swung his legs around on the bed until they were circled around Adrianna. "Come here." Adrianna scooted back until she was leaning against Dante's rock hard chest.

She felt even better when she felt Dante's strong hands on her shoulders and neck as he gently massaged her with soothing strokes. "Hmm, that feels great," she moaned.

"You deserve it," Dante said. He continued his ministrations and slowly the tension eased from her body until he said, "I'm going to have to get back to the city."

"Do you have to go?" Adrianna asked, turning around to face him. She'd gotten used to having Dante beside her. He'd slept next to her every night since he'd been here and she'd felt reassured.

"Adrianna…" Dante hated that she was looking up at him with pleading puppy dog eyes. "I have to. My restaurants can't continue without me indefinitely. Dante's maybe, but Renaissance is still new and I need to keep an eye on it. You know as well as I do that restaurants can have great initial reviews and after a few months service deteriorates. I don't want to see that happen."

Adrianna turned her back to Dante so he wouldn't have to see how disappointed she was. "I understand. I'm a food reviewer, remember?" Not that she had done much reviewing these days, once her father's health had begun to worsen; she'd taken a leave of absence from *Foodies* magazine and only taped *Easy Entertaining.* "I'm going to get ready for bed." Without looking at Dante, she went into the adjoining bathroom and shut the door.

She grabbed a towel to smother the sob that escaped her lips. Dante had every right to leave. He hadn't made her any promises that things had changed between them, that he'd forgiven her for her lies. He'd just been the kind, supportive man she'd always known him to be and stayed by her side in the wake of her father's death. She should be happy to have had this time with him, but it wasn't enough. She loved him. She loved him with all her heart and wanted him back.

Adrianna glanced at herself in the mirror and she looked a mess. Dante certainly wouldn't find her attractive now. Quickly, she turned on the taps and washed her face. When she was done, she put on some moisturizer and brushed her hair until the curls hung in silky waves down her back. She grabbed her nightgown from the hook on the bathroom door, changed and returned to the bedroom.

Dante had removed his jeans and T-shirt which had been a staple during his stay and was bare-chested, wearing only pajama bottoms. Despite how upset she was at his leaving and losing her father, she felt a stirring in her loins for the man she loved. She watched him pull back the covers, turn off the light and slip inside the covers. She would love to luxuriate in his arms, if only for one night.

From across the room, Dante exhaled. Adrianna had emerged from the bathroom wearing a nightie that was sheer enough for him to see her dark brown nipples and the bikini panties she was wearing. The past few days it had been relatively easy to sleep next to her because she'd been grieving, but tonight something was different. He didn't know what it was, but there was definitely sexual tension in the air.

No matter what he and Adrianna had been through last month, he was still as attracted to her as ever. That was the thing, sex was never their problem. Trust was. It was something fundamental in any relationship and Dante just wasn't sure they could ever get it back once that trust was broken. Still, Adrianna was breathtakingly beautiful in the moonlight with her hair in loose waves down her back, her face free of makeup and her body draped in the scrap of lace.

Dante struggled to compose himself. She'd just lost

her father, for goodness' sake; she wouldn't want to be mauled by him because he couldn't control his desire for her.

He held the end of the covers up and Adrianna slipped underneath the cool sheets. She faced Dante, but this time unlike the previous nights, he was completely aware of her physically. Remain calm and detached, he told himself, but when Adrianna wrapped her arm around his middle, pulled him closer and kissed his neck, Dante lost his equilibrium.

"Adrianna." He tried to push her away, but she wrapped one long, sexy thigh across his and inched closer. He knew she had to feel the bulge in his pajamas.

Adrianna tilted her head and pressed her lips against his. Dante tried to resist, but her tongue began tracing the outline of his lips and he lost his resolve and grabbed her buttocks, placing her firmly against his erection.

Their lips met again in a kiss of sweet surrender. Electricity poured through Adrianna's body as if she'd been plugged into a socket. Dante's fingers caressed the curve of her hips, back and up to her shoulders, before pushing the straps of her nightgown down to her waist and then past her hips. He gave each of her breasts a gentle squeeze before laving them with his hot wet tongue. His other hand relieved her of her bikini panties and tossed them aside.

His seductive journey of her breasts elicited a moan from Adrianna, but she refused to be passive. She reached underneath the covers and tugged at his pajama bottoms. Dante lifted his hips and she pushed them lower to his ankles. He drew his mouth away from her beautiful twins long enough to return to masterfully possess her mouth with his lips and tongue.

Dante wanted to lose himself in her, but Adrianna was already pulling away and kneeling to come in contact with his throbbing erection. Her hand softly closed around his member and she began to stroke him with her hands and then with her tongue and then both in tandem. Pressure began to build inside him and her name fell from his lips like a religious chant as his body strained for release from the intimate torture.

"Adrianna, oh, Adrianna," he groaned as she took him to new heights.

When he felt himself on the edge, he quickly flipped her over and eased off the bed to reach for his pants on a nearby chair. Since he'd begun seeing Adrianna, he'd made a habit of keeping plenty of condoms in his wallet and was relieved they were still there.

Adrianna took the condom away from him, helped sheathe his engorged member and took the dominant position by climbing on top of him. She slowly slid down on his hardened shaft until he filled her completely. She needed to be one with him.

For several moments, she didn't move and Dante nearly became unglued. Then she slowly started to rock and Dante relinquished control to her as Adrianna sent him on a mind-bending rollercoaster ride. Her movements were slow and measured so much so that Dante could barely hear her whimpers over his own groans. It was delicious agony and he locked his hands around her hips to accelerate the rhythm. Soon, their cries of release were echoing through the room as they both came together in a huge explosion.

Dante opened his eyes and pulled Adrianna close and when he did he felt her wet tears against his chest. What had he done? Dante felt terrible. How could have let his desires take over his common sense? Adrianna was in no state to make love and he shouldn't have taken advantage. He'd gone too far.

* * *

Adrianna woke up the next morning and felt wonderful. She'd just spent a heavenly night in Dante's arms. It had felt so good and so right, she'd cried tears of joy. She opened her eyes and turned to stretch and found Dante already dressed and packing a suitcase.

When he saw her head lift from the pillow, Dante said, "Listen, about last night…"

"You don't have to say it." Adrianna knew the truth. "I know it was good-bye."

"I didn't mean for that to happen," Dante responded, throwing a T-shirt into the suitcase. "I feel terrible. I took advantage of you in a weak moment."

"You didn't take advantage of me," Adrianna replied, her eyes misty with tears. "I wanted you, too. No, correction, I *needed* you. I needed to be held, to be kissed, to be made love to. I needed to feel human again and you did that. Thank you."

Dante stopped packing and turned around to face her. "I didn't make love to you because I felt sorry for you."

"I know that." Adrianna pulled the sheet from the bed, wrapped it around her bosom and walked toward him. "You made love to me because you wanted to." She took his large hand in hers and kissed it. "Despite everything, there's still something between us, Dante. Something neither one of us can let go."

"I have to go," Dante said, tugging his hand free and closing his suitcase. "I'm sorry to leave…so abruptly, but I think it's best. I don't want to give you any false illusions that anything has changed between us."

"Okay, I understand." Adrianna didn't, but it was his turn to run away and she would have to let him go for now, but she wasn't giving up.

Dante's driver was waiting for him outside and Dante thankfully jumped inside the town car and turned away from the house. On his way out, he'd run into Nigel who'd promised to look after Adrianna in his absence, but Dante had no intention of coming back. Getting involved with Adrianna again was dangerous for his health. He'd stepped up during the funeral and afterward because she'd needed a rock to rely on, but she was getting stronger by the day and would now have to stand on her own two feet. He couldn't—wouldn't—risk his heart again and have Adrianna betray him.

Chapter 15

Once he returned to the city, Dante checked in at Renaissance and Dante's to make sure the restaurants were running smoothly. Outside of a few missing food and supply orders that hadn't been received, both places had been fine in his absence.

He was looking through the books when he received a call from Ian on his cell phone. "Ian, I'm surprised to hear from you," Dante greeted.

"I was hoping you would be available for a drink this evening," Ian replied. "I've already asked Malik and Quentin and they've agreed."

"Is everything okay?" Dante asked. He couldn't remember the last time the four men had drinks together alone. "Is Sage all right?"

"Sage is fine. Are you available at seven?" Ian inquired. "At my penthouse?"

"Yes," Dante answered. "I'm available." He was very curious as to why Ian would call a meeting between the four of them.

"Good, I'll see you then."

Dante wasn't the only one surprised to receive the call. He ran into Quentin at the elevator to the penthouse later that evening.

"Do you know what this is all about?" Quentin asked on the ride up.

"Your guess is as good as mine," Dante replied.

They rang the bell and Ian answered. "Come on in, fellas." Ian motioned them inside. "Malik is already here and is out on the terrace."

Dante glanced at Ian, trying to read his facial expression, but it was impenetrable. He and Quentin followed Ian out on the terrace which had a spectacular view of the Manhattan skyline.

"Beer?" Ian asked

"That would be great, thanks," Dante said.

"None for me." Quentin shook his head.

"I'll be right back." Ian disappeared inside.

"How's Adrianna?" Malik asked, coming forward to join the guys.

"Much better." Dante didn't say more. He didn't want them to know about his lapse in judgment of falling back into bed with Adrianna.

"It was an amazing thing you did for her," Quentin commented. "Standing by her side during the funeral and after."

"Are you guys going to get back together?" Malik inquired.

"Why would you automatically assume that?" Dante asked testily.

"Because you're still in love with her," Malik stated.

Before Dante could respond, Ian returned with two beer bottles and handed one to Dante and kept one for himself.

"So why are we here, Ian?" Dante asked, taking a swig of his beer. He didn't like being called out by Malik and was eager to move on to a different topic of conversation.

"Well." Ian paused and glanced at them. "The three of you are the closest thing Sage has to family so I thought it was only fitting that I should ask you for her hand in marriage."

"Excuse me?" Dante almost spit out his beer.

"It shouldn't come as a shock," Ian replied. "Sage and I love each other and I think I've proved to her and you that I'm not going anywhere. I'm done with my playboy ways. Sage is the only woman for me."

Dante turned away and faced the city. He was about to lose Sage, too. First Quentin, then Malik and now Sage. He would be the only one without a spouse.

But you don't have to be, an inner voice said.

"Yes, you have," Quentin said. "I admit in the beginning I had my doubts about whether you could remain faithful to Sage. Your method of attracting her was far from scrupulous, but you proved me wrong. You've proven you love Sage. You have my blessing."

"I agree," Malik said. "You're a changed man, Lawrence, so you have my blessing as well."

Ian turned to Dante who had remained silent throughout the exchange. He wouldn't ask Sage to marry him without all of their blessings. "Dante? Do I have your blessing?" he asked. "You know I love Sage dearly. I would lay down my life for her."

Dante could understand that because he'd felt the same way about Adrianna once upon a time. The question was would he, could he feel that way again?

"I will make her a good husband," Ian continued. "I

adore her wit, her charm, her beauty, her zest for life and I promise I will never intentionally hurt her."

Dante gave Ian a smile. "Of course you have my blessing, Ian." He may not have found love, but he would not deny that for his little sis. She deserved the best.

"Thank you." Ian shook his hand.

"Welcome to the family," Dante replied.

"Thank you, so then you won't mind my telling you that you are a fool to let Adrianna go," Ian stated bluntly.

"Whoa!" Malik chuckled. "Way to start off on the right foot."

"Ian, this isn't really your business," Dante responded.

"It may not be," Ian stated, "but the two of you have what it takes on and off camera. I walked away from Sage once, but I came to my senses. Maybe all you need is a little time. That's why I'm keeping the offer on the table for *Easy Entertaining*. I'm still committed to the show and as soon as Adrianna is ready to get back to work, I want you both back."

"Ian…" Dante began.

"No buts…just think how happy having this show will make Adrianna after all she's lost. Now she will have something to look forward to."

"You do realize that was a low blow," Dante said.

"Who said the business world was fair?" Ian asked. "Just think about it, because I believe you only want the best for Adrianna."

"You're looking so much better," Madison told Adrianna a few days later when Adrianna came to a movie premiere for an actor Madison was promoting. She hadn't wanted to come, but Madison had insisted she get out of the house. The movie hadn't started yet, so they had a few minutes to catch up.

"Thanks, cuz." Adrianna gave her a hug. "It's been a tough couple of weeks." It had nearly crushed her soul to watch Dante leave, but it had given her a lot of time alone to think. She'd realized that life was too short. She had to fight for what she wanted because tomorrow was not guaranteed. "And thank you for getting me out of the house."

"You're welcome. So, what's next for you?" Madison asked, not that her cousin needed to worry. After the reading of the will, Adrianna had been left with a sizeable fortune and didn't need to work for the rest of her life.

"I'm taking hold of my life," Adrianna stated, "and going after what's mine."

"Whoa!" Madison sat back. She'd never seen her cousin quite this fired up since she'd come back to Manhattan. "What are you going to do?"

"First, I'm going to get my man back," Adrianna said, "and then my cooking show." Sure, she could probably produce her own cooking show now with the money she'd inherited, but then she wouldn't be with Dante.

She'd made a big mistake by keeping the truth from him, but Dante still loved her, of that she was sure. He wouldn't have stayed with her for days after her father died if he didn't. And he sure wouldn't have made love to her with the same passion and emotion he'd once had if he didn't still love her. Now all she had to do was get him to admit it to himself. And she knew exactly where and when to confront him.

"I love this side of you," Madison grinned. "You go, girl." She gave her a high five. "Go get your man. But after the movie."

"Dinner will be served in five minutes," Dante said when the family was gathered in the private wine room of Renaissance for Sunday dinner. It was their indication to head to their seats, but everyone ignored Dante's announcement and continued their conversations. Ian had finally asked Sage to marry him and she'd happily agreed so Avery and Peyton were gushing over Sage's two-and-a-half-carat engagement ring.

Ian as usual was snacking on one of several appetizers Dante had brought in while Quentin and Malik were discussing the New York Knicks game they'd gone to the previous evening.

Since no one seemed to listen, Dante decided to head to the kitchen and peek in on the dinner service. He was on his way there when out of the corner of his eye, he saw a familiar face walking toward him. Adrianna.

"What are you doing here?" Dante asked.

"I came for you," Adrianna responded, her eyes never leaving his face.

She'd come dressed simply in a peasant skirt, embroided tank and sandals, but she was still as sexy as ever. "Adrianna, if you're here about what happened…" Dante began, but she interrupted him.

"It's about that amongst other things."

"What other things?" Dante asked, folding his arms across his chest.

"I want you back," Adrianna stated matter-of-factly.

"You want me back?" Dante repeated the words.

"Yes, and I think you want me, too," Adrianna replied. "Or we wouldn't have made love."

Dante glanced around to make sure no one heard her before grabbing Adrianna's arm and leading her to the coat room nearby, which wasn't being utilized due to the warm weather. "Now is not the time to get into this, Adrianna. My family is here."

"When will be the time?" Adrianna asked. When

Dante didn't answer, she said, "There will never be a good time because you're always going to pull away. I know I hurt you terribly, Dante. I lied to you. Not once, but twice." She held up two fingers. "I didn't tell you I was pregnant and lost our baby and when we found each other again, I still didn't tell you."

"No, you didn't."

"I was wrong, okay?" Adrianna responded, touching her chest. "I fully admit that I should have never kept the truth from you, but life is too short to look back and think about what might have been. If nothing else, my father's death has taught me to seize every moment. Haven't we waited long enough for our happy ending?"

Dante sighed. "I see… So this is all about losing your father and feeling alone. But this, too, shall pass."

Adrianna stomped her foot. "This will not pass, Dante," she returned. "This isn't grief talking. I have always loved you. I met you when I was nineteen years old, you were my first love and I have never stopped loving you. Even when we were apart, you were always in my heart. Please forgive me. I don't want to spend another second without you in my life."

Dante was about to speak when he heard commotion and loud voices. He stepped out of the coat room and saw Malik heading toward the door and Peyton leaning against him holding her large belly. Sage and Ian were right behind them.

"What's going on?" Dante asked, rushing out of the room to open the front door.

"Peyton is in labor." Malik's eyes were wide with excitement. "We're about to have a baby!"

"What can I do?" Dante asked.

"Meet us at the hospital," Malik threw over his shoulder as he rushed her out the door.

Sage walked toward Dante. "Can you believe it?" She laughed. "One minute we're just standing there talking about the ring and the next minute her water is breaking."

"I'll go get the car," Ian said, running out of the restaurant.

"What hospital?" Dante inquired.

"Mount Sinai," Sage said just as Quentin and Adrianna came up behind her with Bella in a baby carrier.

"We'll meet you guys there," Quentin said, heading out the door. "We're going to drop Bella at Avery's mom's, but we'll be there as soon as we can."

"All right, we'll see you there," Dante said.

"There's Ian." Sage pointed to Ian's Porsche Carrera pulling up the curb. He'd taken to driving to Sunday dinner instead of being driven around in his Bentley. "I'll see you there." Sage kissed Dante's cheek on her way out.

Dante stood stunned at the sudden change in events. Malik was about to become a father and then there was… He looked up and saw Adrianna smiling.

"Well, we'd better get moving," she said, "or we're going to miss the big event."

"You're coming?" he asked.

"Of course," Adrianna replied. "I told you. I'm not going anywhere. So are you driving or am I?" She held up her car keys.

"You drive," Dante said and opened the front door. "I'm too nervous."

Hours later, Dante and Adrianna were with the rest of the family in the waiting room. Dante paced the floor back and forth.

"How long is she going to be in there?" Sage inquired.

"Who knows?" Avery smiled, glancing at Quentin. "Could be a few hours or all day." They gave each other knowing smiles as they remembered Avery being in labor with Bella for twelve excruciating hours.

Dante stood leaning against the waiting room wall. He was agitated. Adrianna was sitting down next to Sage and he was at a loss as to what to do. She made a compelling argument that they should seize the moment, but he was scared to take another leap off the ledge. What if he fell straight to the bottom? How could he be sure Adrianna would catch him?

"Are you okay?" Sage asked Adrianna.

"Why would you ask?"

"I just thought it might be a little uncomfortable being here…well, after, you know…you lost your own baby," Sage whispered.

Adrianna nodded. "I'm fine. I've accepted that I lost that child, but there could be more in my future." Adrianna looked in Dante's direction.

Sage glanced at Dante and watched him. "You're here to win him back?" she surmised.

"Yes, if he'll have me."

Sage grabbed Adrianna's hand and squeezed. "Don't give up on him. He loves you. He's just scared."

Adrianna smiled weakly. "Thank you and I won't."

"Do you mind sitting down, brother?" Quentin asked Dante when he began pacing again. "Not only are you wearing a hole in the vinyl, but you're making me dizzy."

"I'm going to get a breath of fresh air," Dante said anxiously, "but I have my phone."

Adrianna watched Dante rush out the room and knew

she had to strike while the iron was hot. Dante was on the fence and he just needed a little push in the right direction. She jumped out of her seat and rushed to follow him outside.

Dante was staring out at midnight sky when he sensed someone behind him. He already knew who it was before he turned around. "You don't give up, do you?"

"I won't give up on us," Adrianna responded, walking toward him. When she reached him, she grabbed both his hands. "I love you, Dante Moore. Please say you'll give us another chance at happiness."

"Adrianna, your words and sentiment are beautiful," Dante replied, pulling his hands out of her grasp. "They really are, but I am not sure I can forgive you. You abandoned me ten years ago without a good-bye. Do you know how much that hurt?"

Adrianna lowered her head.

"It affected me deeply. It made me feel worthless. Like I wasn't good enough for you or anyone because of where I came from."

"I'm sorry I made you feel that way, Dante. I have never cared that you came from humble beginnings. Your struggles, your will and your determination to succeed have made you the man you are, the man I love."

"A man you obviously think very little of," Dante returned. "You popped back into my life just as quickly as you disappeared and allowed me to fall back in love with you only to realize you'd been keeping a terrible secret from me for years."

"A secret I will always regret," Adrianna responded. "Keeping your child away from you would have been wrong and it would have haunted me for the rest of my days. And I'm sorry for it, but that doesn't change the here and now, which is that we love each other. I think

I love you even more because when I was at the lowest point in my life…" Adrianna paused and tears began to stream down her cheeks. "You…you gave me strength. You stood by my side and gave me faith to believe I could go on without my father. I am the woman I am because you loved me. Please forgive me."

Her words finally reached a place deep inside Dante, a part he could no longer hide from. Slowly, Dante reached out to wipe away her tears. "Don't cry, my love," he whispered and bent down to kiss away her tears. "I forgive you." He wrapped Adrianna in his arms and squeezed tight. "And I love you."

Adrianna glanced up through misty eyes. "I love you, too, Dante. And I promise I won't ever lie to you again." She stood on tiptoe and sealed her vow with a persuasive kiss that left little doubt she intended to keep that promise.

Dante was still reeling when he felt his cell vibrate in his pocket. It was a text message from Sage. It's a boy.

Epilogue

"Thanks for joining us on *Easy Entertaining* with the Moores," Dante said, looking straight into the camera and squeezing his wife's shoulder.

"We'll see you next time." Adrianna smiled by his side.

"Cut!" the director yelled. "That was great, guys. Your holiday cooking special is in the can."

Dante gave him a high five as he and Adrianna headed to their dressing room to change clothes.

Easy Entertaining had been on for four months and ratings were slowly soaring which thrilled Ian to no end. He couldn't resist pointing out that he'd "discovered" Dante and Adrianna during the family Sunday dinners.

"I'm so excited we're done taping for the week," Dante replied. "I can't wait to get to the house for some R & R."

He and Adrianna had kept the house in the Hamptons

as their weekend retreat or a place to visit when they needed to get away from the show or the restaurants. They had the entire family up for the Thanksgiving holiday and it had been quite an undertaking considering how their foursome had now expanded to include Quentin, his wife, Avery, and daughter, Bella; Malik, his wife, Peyton, and son, Noah, as well as Sage and her hubby, Ian.

Dante fingered a photograph of the four of them from when they moved out of the orphanage that sat on his dressing-room counter. They'd been young back then, yet full of hopes and dreams. Who would have thought that four orphans who grew up with nothing would end up successful and happily married with children?

"You ready to go home?" Adrianna asked from the doorway. She'd changed into jeans and a cashmere sweater. She was the most stunningly beautiful creature he'd ever laid his eyes on.

"I'm ready, my love," he said, walking to her and bending down to brush his lips tenderly over hers.

* * * * *

Fru·gal·is·ta [froo-*guh-lee*-stuh] *noun*
1. A person who lives within her means and saves money, but still looks good, eats well and lives *fabulously*

THE TRUE STORY OF HOW
ONE TENACIOUS YOUNG WOMAN
GOT HERSELF OUT OF DEBT
WITHOUT GIVING UP HER
FABULOUS LIFESTYLE

NATALIE P. McNEAL

Natalie McNeal opened her credit card statement in January 2008 to find that she was a staggering five figures—nearly $20,000!—in debt. A young, single, professional woman, Natalie loved her lifestyle of regular mani/pedis, daily takeout and nights on the town with the girls, but she knew she had to trim back to make ends meet. The solution came in the form of her *Miami Herald* blog, "The Frugalista Files." Starting in February 2008, Natalie chronicled her journey as she discovered how to maintain her fabulous, single-girl lifestyle while digging herself out of debt and even saving for the future.

THE *Frugalista* FILES

Available wherever books are sold.

HARLEQUIN®

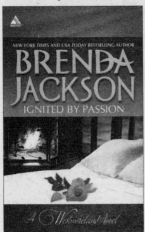
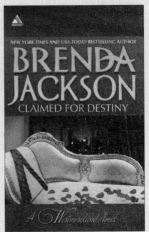

REQUEST YOUR FREE BOOKS!

2 FREE NOVELS
PLUS 2 FREE GIFTS!

KIMANI ROMANCE ™

Love's ultimate destination!

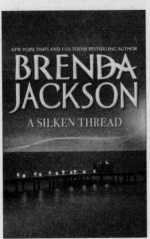